The Theories of Grandfather

Julian Woods

Acknowledgments

i

I wish to thank Professor Jacob Needelman of San Francisco State University for helping me obtain my BA degree in philosophy at the age of fifty-nine years old.

About the Author

The author considers himself an agnostic and tries to convey a religious outlook from an agnostic point of view.

The Theories of Grandfather

Long before I was born, something happened that caused my grandfather to quit going to church. No one spoke of it while my grandfather or grandmother was alive, but the subject came up at grandmother's wake. All of my aunts and uncles gathered together and shared stories of different events that took place while they were growing up. They told stories late into the night, and at some point, my Uncle Junior began to talk about my grandfather's theories, saying that they were what made him a heretic.

According to Uncle Junior, there was a time when people used the phrase, "She got herself pregnant." If a young woman wanted a man to marry her, she would have sex with him and try to get pregnant by him. Afterward, the community would pressure the young man to marry her. But there would always be someone in the community who would defend the young man, claiming the young woman intentionally became pregnant to get him to marry her.

They would say, "She got herself pregnant," which meant she knew what she was doing at the time of conception, while the young man who was having sex with her had no idea she was intentionally getting herself pregnant. Uncle Junior said that grandfather used to say, "The Virgin Mary got herself pregnant by

Zacharias, and Zacharias was the father of both Jesus and John the Baptist."

At one time, my grandfather went to church every Sunday. He was a religious man who studied the Bible and often ended up in a disagreement with someone about how a certain text from the Bible should be understood. One Sunday afternoon, he got into a disagreement about how many children the Virgin Mary gave birth to. Junior Johnson claimed Jesus was the only child the Virgin Mary gave birth to, while Grandfather claimed Jesus had a brother named James, who was one of his disciples. The evening was getting late, and the people who rode to church with my grandfather were waiting for them to stop talking so they could go home. Grandfather and Junior Johnson agreed to continue their conversation the following week after the Sunday school service.

That week, Grandfather went to the Los Angeles library after work and looked up everything he could find on how many children the Virgin Mary gave birth to. If there was anything written about the Virgin Mary outside of what was in the Bible, he wanted to read it; he seemed obsessed with proving his point. During that time, Grandfather had a dream, and when he awoke, he claimed he knew who the biological father of Jesus Christ was. When Sunday came around, everyone in the family went to church early that week.

Junior Johnson was the son of the church's pastor, and he was studying to become an ordained minister. Members of the church expected him to take his father's place as pastor one day. He taught Sunday school in the sanctuary before church services, hoping the children would grow up to become members of his future congregation and remember being taught the Bible by him.

There was a short break, lasting about half an hour, between Sunday school and the church service. As soon as Sunday school was over, Grandfather was waiting to continue the argument. He went up to Junior Johnson, told him the names of Jesus' brothers, and pointed out that Jesus had more than one sister.

Grandfather was so busy talking that he didn't notice the parents who had come to pick up their children from Sunday school. Once they had their children, they didn't leave; they wanted to stay and hear what Grandfather was saying. Junior Johnson noticed how everyone seemed interested, so he told them to grab a Bible and open it to the book of Matthew, where they could read the passages and see what Grandfather was talking about.

At that time, Reverend Johnson walked in, so Junior turned the floor over to his father, who knew much more about the Bible than he did. Grandfather named all of Jesus' brothers mentioned in Matthew (13:55)—James, Joses, Simon, and Judas—then asked Reverend Johnson if he agreed that Jesus had brothers and sisters.

The Reverend claimed Joseph was years older than Mary and was a widower who had children by a previous marriage before he became engaged to Mary, so all of Jesus' brothers and sisters were children Joseph fathered by his first wife. Grandfather disagreed and showed him a passage near the beginning of the book of Luke, which said Jesus was the Virgin Mary's firstborn son. "If Jesus was her only child, it would have said 'only son,' not 'firstborn son,'" said Grandfather. He insisted the brothers and sisters mentioned in the book of Matthew were the children of the Virgin Mary, then went on to share his version of the conception of Jesus, which had come to him in a dream earlier that week.

"Jesus and John the Baptist were born six months apart. Elisabeth, the mother of John the Baptist, was a first cousin of the Virgin Mary. When she was six months pregnant, the Virgin Mary came to visit her and stayed in the household of Elisabeth and Zacharias for three months. Mary came to take care of Elisabeth while she was pregnant. When Mary arrived, she saw all the fuss about the child that was gonna be born. Zacharias, the father of the child, was a priest; I figure he must've been the high priest or head priest in those days. But this child was gonna be special; it was gonna be holy. The child would grow up to be 'great in the sight of the Lord.'

"Now, according to the book of Luke, the Virgin Mary was pregnant with Jesus when she arrived to care for Elisabeth. I don't think she was. It doesn't make sense to send one pregnant woman to take care of another one. I believe she saw how much attention Elisabeth was getting and wanted to have the exact same child Elisabeth was going to give birth to. So, the Virgin Mary got herself pregnant by Zacharias; during that time, Zacharias was silent and couldn't speak until John the Baptist was born.

"Now I have a theory, and my theory is that the same person who was the father of John the Baptist was also the father of Jesus Christ. That would explain why Jesus and John the Baptist were born six months apart."

"That's absurd," said Reverend Johnson.

"Just think about it," said Grandfather. "Elisabeth was six months pregnant when the Virgin Mary came to see her. The Virgin Mary stayed for three months and left; when she left, she was three months pregnant."

"Let's stick to the scripture," said Reverend Johnson. "According to scripture, the angel Gabriel was sent by God to the city of Galilee, where Mary was. And he told Mary she would conceive a son who would be called Jesus. Mary asked Gabriel how that could be, seeing she was still a virgin. Gabriel told her, 'The Holy Ghost shall come upon thee, and the power of the Highest shall overshadow thee, for with God, nothing shall be impossible.' Mary was made pregnant by the Holy Spirit. Now, some say the Holy Spirit planted a seed in Mary's womb, and the seed was from God and of God. How the Holy Spirit did this is not the issue; the point is she was made pregnant by the Holy Spirit."

Grandfather wasn't buying it; he didn't believe Mary had gotten pregnant by the Holy Spirit. He believed he'd received divine insight from the dream he had showing him how Jesus was conceived. Grandfather realized he had to stick to the scriptures to win his argument. Never mind who the father of Jesus was, he thought; he had to get back to the number of children the Virgin Mary gave birth to before she died. If he could prove the Virgin Mary gave birth to at least seven children before she died, it would not seem likely she was a virgin when Jesus was born.

"Okay," said Grandfather, "tell me this: according to the scriptures, how many children did the Virgin Mary give birth to before she died?"

"Well," replied Reverend Johnson, "exactly which scriptures of the Bible are you referring to?"

Grandfather opened his Bible to the book of Matthew and pointed to the thirteenth chapter, verses fifty-five and fifty-six. He showed it to the Reverend and said, "I'm referring to these scriptures right here."

The Reverend had his own Bible; he could have easily read it from Grandfather's Bible, but it didn't take long for him to look it up in his own Bible. The Reverend didn't mean any offense by not reading it from Grandfather's Bible; he did it with everyone.

Whatever scripture was in question, he wanted to read it from his own personal best friend—his Bible. The Reverend read the scripture and said, "If you notice, in verse fifty-five, it says, 'Is not this the carpenter's son?' Now, we all know Jesus was not the son of Joseph, but Joseph was the one who raised him. So Joseph was the carpenter mentioned in verse fifty-five. The same thing applies to his brothers and sisters; these were children who grew up with Jesus. They may have been fathered by Joseph from his first wife before he married the Virgin Mary, but as far as the church is concerned, the Virgin Mary only gave birth to one child: Jesus."

"So, according to the church, the Virgin Mary lived her entire life as a virgin and was a virgin when she died?" asked Grandfather.

"That's right," said Reverend Johnson.

"I don't believe it's possible for a spirit to get a woman pregnant, but I do believe the Virgin Mary gave birth to these children whose names are in the book of Matthew," said Grandfather.

"You can believe whatever you choose to believe, but the words written in the Bible are the truth," said the Reverend.

Grandfather yelled, "The words written in the Bible are the names of the brothers and sisters of Jesus."

Grandfather had become angry. He felt the facts were on his side, and the Reverend completely ignored the facts to make it look as if Grandfather was the one who didn't know what the truth was. The Reverend told Grandfather he had to get ready for the church services, which would start in less than fifteen minutes, and he turned and walked away. Everyone there followed the Reverend as he left the building where they taught Sunday school—everyone except Junior Johnson.

Junior Johnson, the Reverend's oldest child, couldn't help taking advantage of the situation. He and Grandfather had known each other since elementary school and had both moved to California from Texas. Sometime in the middle of the 20th century, there was a migration of Black families out of Texas. Black people had lived in Texas since before it was a state in the United States of America, and most of them were proud of their Texas heritage. But at one time, the mines closed down, and the people who worked in the mines couldn't find work, so they went wherever they could find work.

A number of Black people who worked in the mines were able to find work in Southern California during the middle of the 20th century. Southern California was the fastest-growing area of the United States, and those who found work there wrote back to their family and friends that there were plenty of jobs in California.

This ended up causing a migration of Black people from Texas to California. For the most part, the vast majority of them did find work, and when they looked for a place to stay, they chose areas near their friends and family. There were redlined districts and areas where Black people were not supposed to look for housing, but the point is that the Black people who moved to Southern California from Texas mostly all lived in the same area.

The area became a community known as Little Texas because most of the people who lived there were from Texas. Grandfather and the Johnson family had known each other in Texas before everyone moved to California, and once in California, everyone from Texas became a member of Reverend Johnson's church. That is, everyone from Texas who went to church. Now was Junior Johnson's chance to get back at Grandfather for trying to say the Virgin Mary was not a real virgin.

Junior Johnson tried to be as inconspicuous as possible as he slowly eased his way up to Grandfather and said, "Ya know, opinions are like ass holes—everybody's got one, and next to my opinion, your opinion stinks." He then followed everyone else on their way to the main chapel, where Sunday services were about to get underway.

Grandfather put on his hat, turned, and walked out of the building. While everyone else who left was heading toward the main building where the chapel was located, Grandfather was walking in a different direction—he was heading toward the street. Grandmother caught up with him and tried to calm him down. She wanted him to go back to church, but Grandfather told her he would wait in the car until church services were over.

"You can't sit outside in the car while everyone else is in church," Grandmother said.

Grandfather happened to look up and see the local bus coming down the street. It was several blocks away, and he had plenty of time to get to the bus stop before the bus arrived.

"You're right," said Grandfather. He reached in his pocket, pulled out the car keys, handed them to her, and said, "I'll see yah when yah get home." He walked to the nearby bus stop, caught the bus home, and from that day until he died, he never went back to church. Although Grandfather never returned to church, he still believed in God and continued to wonder about certain passages in the Bible.

Eunuchs

One of the passages in the New Testament that confused Grandfather was Matthew Chapter 19, verses 11 and 12.

Jesus said unto them, "Not everyone can receive this saying, but only those to whom it is given.

For there are eunuchs which were born from their mother's womb: and there are some eunuchs which were made eunuchs of men: And there are eunuchs who have made themselves eunuchs for the kingdom of heaven's sake.

He that is able to receive it, let him receive it."

Grandfather always wondered what Jesus was talking about when he spoke of "eunuchs for the kingdom of heaven" and "Let he who is able to receive this saying receive it." At first, Grandfather thought, "Let he who is able to receive this saying receive it" meant that a person who had knowledge of what Jesus was talking about would understand what Jesus meant about eunuchs for the kingdom of heaven and would be able to accept what Jesus was saying, thereby receiving it as something they already understood.

The more Grandfather thought about it, the more he came to believe Jesus might have meant something else. Suppose Jesus was saying that the eunuchs who were made eunuchs for the kingdom of heaven were able to receive something spiritual by becoming eunuchs for the kingdom of heaven, and that those who were able to receive whatever it was the eunuchs for the kingdom of heaven received, "let him receive it." No matter what anyone says, we will never know. The only way for us to know for sure is if we could ask Jesus and get him to tell us exactly what he meant.

Grandfather knew that years ago, the Catholic Church used to castrate young boys about the age of eleven or twelve years old, supposedly for the sake of causing them to sing with a high voice in the church choir. Other than that, he felt he knew very little about eunuchs, so he went to the library to read up on them and find out what Jesus meant about young men making themselves eunuchs for the kingdom of heaven.

There was very little he could find about eunuchs that was written by the Catholic Church, but he found a book called Hidden Power: The Palace Eunuchs of Imperial China. According to the book, "Nowhere were eunuchs of such great and long-continuing historical significance as in the palace of imperial China." Eunuchs were used to guard the harem of the Emperor of China, and at times, they had sex with the Emperor and were considered to be not just guards but part of the Emperor's harem. They were also used as advisors, which placed them in a position of having influence on the Emperor of China.

Eunuchs were used to educate and look after the heir to the throne; they would pretty much raise the future Emperor of China. Once the heir to the throne became the Emperor, the eunuchs who raised him would serve as his advisors. In some cases, the heir to the throne would become the Emperor while he was still a child, and eunuchs would literally run the empire of China.

At the end of the Ming Dynasty, there were 70,000 eunuchs in China. The eunuchs of India, known as the "Hijra," number as many as 200,000. There were an estimated 11,000 eunuchs in Persia between the rule of Cyrus and Darius the First. Cyrus, the ruler of Persia, appointed eunuchs to every position close to him at the Persian court. In every major culture or civilization on earth, there were people who became eunuchs; some were forced to become eunuchs, while others became eunuchs of their own free will. But in the Hebrew culture, it was outlawed for a person to become a eunuch. The Roman Emperor Julian wrote about having a political struggle against the eunuchs of Rome because they had become so powerful that their influence was able to control the Roman government. Eunuchs served as advisors to rulers of nations; they served as generals of armies and as governors of provinces.

Some scholars believe that Joseph in the Bible was sold into Egypt as a eunuch, that he was castrated by the Ishmaelites (Genesis 37: verses 27-28) before being taken into Egypt to be sold as a slave.

Although Joseph ended up with a wife and children, it is common practice for a eunuch of great social status to have a wife and children. Eunuchs who accumulated a great deal of wealth would marry a woman, and afterward, the wife would become pregnant by her husband's brother. The child would be raised as the eunuch's biological child and would inherit the eunuch's wealth when he died. The eunuch would see his brother's child as the closest thing he could have to an offspring in terms of blood relations.

Grandfather read about how people were made into eunuchs for reasons other than to sing in the choir with a high voice or guard the harem of a powerful ruler. It was as if some of the eunuchs, not all but some of them, possessed a superior intellect compared to the intellect of a normally intelligent person; one might say an intellect superior to that of an intellectual. It was said some could communicate without using words to speak; they were able to use mental telepathy, and in some instances, they were able to look into the future and predict a certain outcome. Grandfather came to believe eunuchs created their own secret societies, which sprang from a monastery founded by St. Lazarus in the eleventh century. He believed that the same secret society that sprang from a monastery run by eunuchs was still in existence today and was able to manipulate people and organizations at the apex of the society we live in.

While doing his research, he came across something written in the late 1960s by a person named Stephen Byrd. It was an essay about eunuchs being represented on television without the general public knowing about it. In his essay, he writes of two different television shows during the 1960s that aired on two different channels but were on at the same time. Both television shows lasted one hour. The name of one show was Lost in Space, and the other was Star Trek. Each television show had a central character who was supposed to be a eunuch. In Lost in Space, the character called Dr. Smith is a eunuch; in Star Trek, the character called Mr. Spock is a eunuch. The two shows came on at the same time, and if you were a eunuch or someone who knew about it, you'd watch Lost in Space for the first half hour, then during the commercial break, which came on at about the middle of the hour, you'd change the channel and watch Star Trek for the remaining half hour until the show ended. Sometimes, you'd watch Star Trek first, then switch to Lost in Space. There was supposed to be some kind of esoteric message or story that came in two parts: Dr. Smith gave the first part of the message, and Mr. Spock would complete the second part of the message. Sometimes, the message would be a true story about something that was going on at that time, which involved real people who were eunuchs.

The two characters in the television shows were supposed to represent the contrasting images of eunuchs. Dr. Smith was always afraid of something and would scream like a woman. He seemed more sexually attracted to the boy Will Robinson than any of the women; he was always scheming on his own behalf and cared only about himself.

Mr. Spock, on the other hand, showed no emotion at all, was considered "asexual," and was more intelligent than the most intelligent human being. He was an intellectual of the highest order. Mr. Spock was second in command, and that was symbolic of the position of a eunuch at the height of his ambition. A eunuch would rise to a position of being second to the person in charge, thereby always being in a position to tell the person in charge what needs to be done, while not being the one who bears the responsibility of what needs to be done. Mr. Spock was symbolic of the eunuch who became a general, a governor, or a eunuch who told a ruler what he needed to do, whereas Dr. Smith was symbolic of the eunuch who guarded the harem, sang in the choir, and portrayed a woman in a stage play when women weren't allowed to act on stage.

Stephen Byrd had also claimed to have met the founder and president of a major record company during the 1960s. He said the two of them hit it off upon first meeting, and the founder of the record company, Mr. Gordon Detroit, told him a story about a castrati who sang for Detroit Records. At the time, the young man in question was the lead singer of a singing group that performed for Detroit Records. The group was made up of five Black youths who were teenagers, all under the age of eighteen. The lead singer of the group was only eleven years old when they had their first hit record, which caused the singing group to become very popular. The father of the eleven-year-old lead singer had a gambling debt with some gangsters. He owed them a large amount of money, which he didn't have, and the gangsters threatened to kill him if he did not pay up.

Gordon Detroit made a deal with the young man's father to pay off his gambling debt on the condition that his son, whose nickname was Peter Pan, would become a castrati who would sing for Detroit Records. The father agreed, and Peter Pan became a eunuch at the age of eleven and a half years old (not the fictional character Peter Pan of Neverland, but the eleven-year-old Black child who was the lead singer of a singing group). This happened about the same time the singing group was making their second album for Detroit Records. When Peter Pan grew up, his lifestyle fit the profile of a eunuch, and he was often questioned about his sexual preference.

When Grandfather read about the singer Peter Pan being castrated between eleven and twelve years old, it caused him to realize something. He had read that in ancient times, young boys had to be castrated at just the right age, which was about eleven or twelve years old. At that age, their hormonal glands had not fully developed, and a person had to be castrated right after their hormonal glands started to develop but before they could fully develop. If they were castrated too early, their hormonal glands would not have developed enough; if they were castrated too late, their hormonal glands would have already developed past a certain point, making them too developed.

After they had been castrated, it took three days for them to know if the operation was a success. In cases where the operations were not a success, the boy would be unable to urinate, and he would die an agonizing death. After years of doing this, someone came up with the idea of inserting a small, thin, hollow straw into the urethra until it passed the point where the testicles had been removed. From then on, once a person had been castrated, they would be able to urinate because the hollow straw inserted into the urethra would prevent the wound, or the urethra, from closing up. Afterward, they became far more successful at turning boys into castrati.

About this time, Grandfather had a dream about what happened to Jesus when he was twelve years old. In the dream, Grandfather went to a movie, and in the movie, the parents of Jesus (Mary and Joseph) would take trips to Jerusalem once a year from where they lived in Galilee.

One year, when Jesus was about twelve years old, they took the trip. They were not alone and traveled in a caravan that contained all of their relatives who made the trip to Jerusalem. Jesus was Mary and Joseph's oldest child, and while Mary and Joseph were looking after the younger brothers and sisters of Jesus, they thought Jesus was somewhere in the caravan with his aunts and uncles when they left Jerusalem to return to Galilee.

Jesus, at age twelve, remained in Jerusalem, but he was not alone; there was an adult whom Jesus had known who was a member of the caravan. This adult introduced Jesus to a boy who was six months older than Jesus when they first arrived. The boy was to be Jesus' guide and show him the city. They became best friends in a matter of hours, and Jesus was having the time of his life with his newfound friend. When it came time for the caravan Jesus had come to Jerusalem with to go back to Galilee, the adult who introduced Jesus to his newfound friend showed up. He told Jesus he had a choice to make: he could stay in Jerusalem with his newfound friend and become like his friend. Then he explained how his newfound friend had had an operation that removed his testicles and made him special, and he believed that God wanted Jesus to give his testicles to God and become a eunuch for the kingdom of heaven, making him and his newfound friend brothers in a special way.

Jesus chose to stay in Jerusalem and become a eunuch for the kingdom of heaven and a brother of his newfound friend. The three of them went back to the caravan and made sure Mary and Joseph and all of Jesus' relatives saw him running around playing when it came time for the caravan to leave. When the caravan left to go back to Galilee, the three of them slipped away. The adult who Jesus knew took him to a place where a group of men who were doctors had gathered to discuss a new procedure. When Jesus showed up, they believed God had sent him to them to perform the operation on.

Mary and Joseph had gone a full day on their journey back to Galilee before they realized Jesus was missing. When Mary and Joseph went to look for him, no one had seen him since they left Jerusalem, so they left Jesus' brothers and sisters, along with their pet dog, in the care of their relatives in the caravan, and Mary and Joseph set off for Jerusalem in search of their oldest child, Jesus. The whole time they traveled back to Jerusalem, Mary kept telling Joseph, "Just wait till I get my hands on him." Joseph kept telling Mary to calm down; it wasn't doing her any good to get angry over something they had no control over.

After three days, they found Jesus. He was in a temple, sitting in the midst of doctors. There was a reason why they found him in the midst of doctors. One of the doctors there had performed the surgery on Jesus, causing him to become a eunuch, and it turned out so well that he had all of his colleagues assembled to witness how well it turned out. In Grandfather's dream, there had been a difference in the consciousness of Jesus before and after he became a eunuch. After Jesus became a eunuch, his awareness seemed to excel, and he acquired an understanding that no twelve-year-old should be able to comprehend. Mary and Joseph realized this and were amazed at his understanding when they found him.

Grandfather awoke from the dream and wondered to himself: When Jesus was twelve years old, he turned up missing for three days. Three days was the time it took for a castration to be successful. And when they found him, he was in the midst of doctors who were astonished. Could these doctors mentioned in the New Testament have performed an operation on Jesus, causing him to become a eunuch? Is that why Jesus was missing for three days? Grandfather realized that if Jesus were a eunuch, it would not be written in the Bible. He wondered if it was written in the Bible whether Jesus had a beard or not. Just because someone paints a picture of Jesus with a beard doesn't mean he really had one. Did Jesus have blond hair, blue eyes, and a white complexion? Grandfather didn't think so.

But just about every picture he had ever seen of Jesus was like that. The only picture of a black-skinned Jesus or any dark-complexioned Jesus was a painting or picture that was sold on the street by a black street vendor in the 'black community. But in every white church, there's a painting of a white Jesus, and how many black churches have a painting of Jesus with a dark complexion and nappy hair?

While studying at the library, he learned that the paintings and pictures he had seen of Jesus Christ were based on Cesare Borgia's image painted as Jesus. So, for Grandfather, the whole issue rested on whether or not Jesus had a beard. Grandfather knew that whether Jesus had a beard or not didn't determine if Jesus was a eunuch, but it was something to base his belief upon until he found some kind of fact that would prove or disprove Jesus being a eunuch.

The fact that not one page of the New Testament was written by Jesus bothered my grandfather. How come we have absolutely nothing that was written by Jesus? Jesus was a carpenter, and although carpenters have knowledge of numbers, you don't have to know how to read or write in order to be a carpenter. Back in those days, the elite were the only people who knew how to read. But Jesus knew how to read because he read the scripture in the temple.

So if Jesus could read and write, how come he didn't write anything, or the Virgin Mary, or Joseph, or John the Baptist, or Zacharias, the father of John the Baptist? We know Zacharias could read because he wrote the name John during the time when he couldn't speak. It seemed odd Zacharias didn't write anything about the angel Gabriel coming to visit him and telling him he would have a son in his old age, and his son would grow up to be John the Baptist. Zacharias was struck dumb by the angel Gabriel and couldn't speak until his son was born, and for nine months, he had to write in order to communicate with people. So, for nine months, he could have written about what happened that caused him not to speak, yet we have nothing known to mankind that is in the handwriting of Zacharias.

Grandfather wanted to know about the people who wrote about Jesus; or rather, he wanted to know exactly who it was that wrote about Jesus in the New Testament.

By now, people who worked in the library were used to seeing grandfather. He knew his way around in terms of what kind of books were on which shelf, which aisle, and how to use the card catalog and the reference section of the library. It seemed the books he needed to read the most were always in the reference section, which meant he couldn't take the book out of the library. Grandfather used to say he did not find God in church; he found God in the library when he read what was written about God before the Bible was written, and in the library, grandfather learned a lot about the early history of Christianity. He learned that after Jesus died, his followers—the people who heard him preach—would meet in different groups to discuss Jesus. Their main topic seemed to be: What did Jesus mean by the kingdom of God?

The concept of the kingdom of God was the basis for the formation of different groups who would meet. Each of these groups differed, but a common feature was the practice of having meals together. These groups of people who were the followers of Jesus existed before any of the books in the New Testament were written. They created the synoptic gospels and were the founders of Christianity. The followers of Jesus were divided into groups, much like we have different kinds of Christians today, and for years, they would talk about the life and teachings of Jesus until one of the groups decided to write them down.

Soon, or years after, another group wrote down their version of the life and teachings of Jesus, and one by one, each group of the followers of Jesus had their own version of what happened. But none of them were there when Jesus walked the earth. By the time they wrote the first story about Jesus, he had been dead for at least sixty years, and what they wrote down was what had been passed down as oral tradition over the last sixty years. That was the first book written about Jesus, which, years and years later, became known as the Book of Mark.

So the Book of Mark belonged to one group, the Book of Matthew belonged to another group, the Book of Luke belonged to another group, and the Book of John belonged to yet another group. Before the Book of Mark, there was no story of the life of Jesus written down. The followers who wrote Mark took many little sayings and stories about Jesus that were available from earlier traditions and then used them to create an image of Jesus like the one in the New Testament (which was written after the Roman-Jewish War about 66–70 AD).

The Mark to whom the gospel is attributed is a legendary figure from the second century. In 130 AD, the Bishop of Hierapolis named Mark the author of the gospel and interpreter of Peter, as if Mark had written it from Peter's memory with notes as his secretary. A Mark is mentioned as Peter's son in the first epistle of Peter, but most scholars believe the epistles of Peter were not written by Peter and are a pseudonymous document from the second century. The name of the authors of the Book of Mark is unknown, and almost all of the Book of Mark is found in the Book of Matthew. Both Matthew and Luke rely heavily on what is written in Mark.

The Book of John was written between 90 and 130 AD. It was the last of the synoptic gospels to be written and is ascribed to have been written by the apostle John, but it was not (nor was the Book of Revelations written by John of Patmos). Scholars believe the Christian community that wrote the Book of John developed its own view of Jesus as a manifestation of God on earth, unlike the Jesus in Mark, Matthew, or Luke.

The Book of Luke was written in the early second century, seventy-five or more years after the time of Jesus. It is the only book in the New Testament that tells of the birth of Jesus or the story of Jesus missing for three days when he was twelve years old. This was the part of the New Testament that grandfather was most concerned about. How did Luke come to know the story of Jesus' birth (and what might have been his castration) some seventy-five years after his death?

Grandfather found out that Luke was thought to have derived some of his material from the oral tradition of asking people. He also drew from the teachings of Jesus, which came from the followers who wrote the book of Matthew, and modern scholars agree that Luke used the gospel of Mark as one of his sources. Grandfather discovered that most of the writings in the New

Testament were either written anonymously and later assigned to a person in the past or written as a pseudonym for someone thought to have been important. There was a word Grandfather learned called "pseudepigrapha," which describes how both the Old and New Testaments were written.

Grandfather claimed that, according to the scholar Burton L. Mack, the early followers of Jesus thought of him as a teacher of wisdom and a figure of moral authority. At some point during the 50s and 60s of the first century, the scribes in the Jesus movement added prophetic and judgmental material in an attempt to transform Jesus into an apocalyptic prophet.

Grandfather came to believe the three days Jesus was missing at age twelve may have been something made up. Luke may not have written it, but the group of followers known as the "Q" group probably wrote it. If Luke did indeed write it, he had no way of knowing if it was true. Luke could only have written what someone told him about Jesus seventy-five years after Jesus had died. So, no one Luke talked to was an eyewitness to what happened. The birth of Jesus happened over a hundred years before Luke wrote about it, so how did Luke learn about the birth of Jesus?

Grandfather came to the conclusion that scribes made up stories about Jesus they wanted us to believe, so we would live our lives according to the way they believed was the best way for us to live. The real Jesus was just a man, whereas the Jesus they wrote about in the New Testament had become the Son of God. One was a man; the other was a myth.

Grandfather had to choose between his faith, which he had believed in all his life, and what the facts had uncovered and made clear to him as the truth. He began to look at religion from his own personal view of how he saw God. He used to say, "In order to have a government, you have to have at least two people, but you only need one person in order to have a religion." That was when Grandfather decided he would come up with his very own religion, one that would allow him to worship God as he saw fit and not the way the church claimed he should worship God.

Most religions have people go out and get others to join them; otherwise, their religion will die out. Grandfather did not believe in proselytizing or trying to convert others into accepting his religious beliefs. If getting other people to believe what you believe meant keeping your religion from dying out, then Grandfather's religion would die along with him when he passed away. It was his and only his belief; if someone else happened to believe in the same things he believed in, it did not mean they were going to start a church—it just meant they saw eye to eye.

Above all, Grandfather's religious beliefs were that he should respect other people's religious beliefs and not argue or debate whatever he disagreed with about their beliefs. He tried to realize that a person's religion is simply what they believe and is not based on fact but on belief. Most people believe their religion is based on fact but will not agree with you as to what the facts are.

If Grandfather was going to have his own religion, he had to confront two basic questions: Does God exist, and if so, where did God come from?

In The Beginning
(Or The Ontological Argument)

Where did God come from? If God created the universe, who created God? In order for God to create the universe, it would mean God had to exist when nothing else existed because the universe consists of everything. If the universe did not exist, then there was nothing in existence, and that includes God.

Grandfather had pondered the question, "Where did God come from?" for many years. He believed everything that exists can be traced back to the point where it came into existence. So, where did God come from? Grandfather believed that before the Big Bang took place, there was only chaos and no order. The universe was made up of gases and matter with a huge amount of increasing combustion until the gases ignited, and an explosion took place known as the Big Bang, which caused the creation of the universe as we know it today.

God did not exist before the Big Bang; for one thing, there was no consciousness before the Big Bang. Consciousness did not come into existence until after the Big Bang, and God cannot exist without consciousness. If God were to exist without consciousness, God would be unconscious. If God had existed before the Big Bang, the Big Bang would have killed God because God would have been blown up like everything else when the Big Bang happened. After the Big Bang took place, a rotational movement came into existence, which required an order that did not exist before. It was as if movement was the key to understanding the universe and how everything in it is somehow based on the movement of itself or the movement of something else. That is how the universe came into existence and is able to sustain life.

Before the Big Bang, there was no order. The movement that existed before the Big Bang was the collision of objects bumping into each other in a haphazardly random manner. The need for order was guided by a force that put things where they needed to be. This force did not have a name, did not have consciousness, but whatever was needed to create the universe, this force was able to bring it about. Try to imagine a blind person sitting at a table, and the table they're sitting at is the universe and everything in it. Now, imagine a crossword puzzle with millions of pieces is dumped onto the table in front of the blind person. The blind person sitting at the table cannot see what the pieces look like, but they feel what shape each piece is like. One by one, they put pieces of the puzzle together based on the feel of how the shapes fit together. They put oxygen and hydrogen together, and water comes into existence. In this way, they put other pieces of the puzzle together until consciousness comes into existence. Exactly how or when consciousness came into existence, Grandfather was never able to find out, and he wondered if there had to be some kind of life form in order for consciousness to exist. As big as the universe is, he believed consciousness did not need a life form in order to exist, and that consciousness only needed a form of energy in order to exist. After consciousness came into existence, that which we call God was created. Grandfather named this force that created God "The Creator," and he saw it as what caused the creation of the universe as we know it today.

Grandfather had no idea when, where, or how consciousness came into existence, but if he could find out when consciousness first came into existence, he would be able to find the origins of God and discover how God came into existence. There are many who believe God and the Creator are one and the same being and that God created the universe. According to my grandfather, that's just not true. God and the Creator are two different beings. God has consciousness; the Creator does not have consciousness. God was created by the Creator, the force that created the universe. And on that note, may the force be with you.

Grandfather had read in Greek mythology, "God did not create the universe; the universe created God." While reading Greek mythology, Grandfather came across the Oracle of Delphi and the saying, "Know thyself." Grandfather changed it around and would say, "To know thyself is to know God."

Grandfather believed a human being was the walking, talking, living, breathing temple of God and that the spirit of God existed inside each and every living human being. He claimed there is a spark of divinity inside each and every one of us, and that spark of divinity is like a cord or a conduit that allows God to exist inside our physical body.

There are times when God will speak to us from inside other people without them knowing it, and there are times when God will speak to other people from inside of us without our knowing it. But what is God? If you were to ask one hundred people from all over the world to give you their definition of God, you might well end up with one hundred different definitions of what God is.

There are people who go to church every Sunday who believe in God, and there are people who never go to church who believe in God. There are atheists who wouldn't hurt a fly but don't believe in the existence of God, and there are agnostics who believe in something but do not believe in what the church or Bible says as the definitive authority on the definition of God.

Grandfather considered himself an agnostic because he believed in God but did not believe in God the way the church or the Bible wanted people to believe in God. On one occasion, my aunt Ada asked my grandfather to give her his definition of God. Grandfather paused for a moment, looked up at the ceiling as if he were searching outside himself for an answer, and scratched his cheek. The room became silent as everyone waited to hear him give Aunt Ada an answer.

After a short while, he began to speak: "I see God as a spiritual being that does not have a physical body but has a consciousness that is the highest level of consciousness known to man, or the highest level of consciousness in existence. At times, I see God as a spiritual being that longs for the physical body of a human being, while human beings long for the consciousness of God."

Yakou

Grandfather wasn't the only person who had his own religion; there was a black man named Yakou who lived in the neighborhood. He was much younger than my grandfather, and like my grandfather, he read a lot, though Yakou didn't go to the library as often as my grandfather did.

Yakou was known for owning a lot of books and claimed that most Christians in the United States used the King James Bible and had no idea there was more than one Bible. In fact, there are quite a few different Bibles. One of his favorites was the Hebrew Bible, and he would often point out differences between the Hebrew Bible and the King James Bible. He would claim, "In the King James Bible, God is mentioned as The Most High God but is not mentioned by the name of Elohim, whereas in the Hebrew Bible, Elohim is the Most High God."

According to Yakou, monotheism started with Abraham. Before Abraham, the Hebrew people worshiped more than one god. "If you look at a map of Abraham's journey, he started out from the city of Ur, which is in Mesopotamia, and went north to Haran, which today would be the southeast part of Turkey. From there, he journeyed south until he ended up in Egypt. In those days, just about every major city had its own god the people would worship. So you have to realize that just about everywhere

Abraham went, there was a different god the people were worshiping.

There was a god to make it rain, a god to make their crops grow; there was a god of the underworld, a god of the sky, and so on and so forth. Abraham decided he would worship the Most High God, which was Elohim, and no other god. Elohim was also known as El The Bull God and was the father of many other gods, one of which was Baal (who was also a bull god). In the book of Genesis 14:18-22, the Hebrew Bible uses the word Elohim, whereas the King James Bible uses "The Most High God" in place of the word Elohim.

Later on, Moses leaves Egypt because he killed an Egyptian. He goes to Midian, where God speaks to him from a burning bush, and in Exodus 6:3, God says to Moses, "I appeared unto Abraham, unto Isaac, and unto Jacob, by the name of God Almighty, but by my name Yahweh was I not known."

It is in the land of Midian that God tells Moses his name is Yahweh. In the Hebrew Bible, it says God's name is Yahweh, while in the King James Bible, it says God's name is Jehovah. The important thing is that Abraham worshiped God under the name Elohim, and Elohim was a Canaanite god worshiped by both Canaanites and Israelites alike. The name Yahweh shows up in the land of Midian, which is south of Canaan and east of Egypt, near the top of the Red Sea. This would indicate that the god Elohim came from Canaan, and the god Yahweh came from Midian.

While Moses was up on Mount Sinai receiving the Ten Commandments, the people waiting for him to come down from the mountaintop thought he was taking too long and got tired of waiting. They went back to worshiping God as Elohim, who is also a Canaanite god, and they had Moses' brother Aaron build them a golden calf to worship. The golden calf was in the form of a bull, which was a symbol of El Elohim, also known as The Bull God. The people figured if Aaron built the golden calf, there was not much Moses could say if his brother was the one responsible for re-establishing their old religion, the worship of Elohim, the Most High God.

When Moses came down from the mountaintop with the Ten Commandments and saw the people worshiping Elohim, he became furious. It was the god Yahweh from Midian who led the people out of bondage from Egypt, not Elohim, whom they worshiped while they were in bondage in Egypt. Moses tried his best to stop the people from worshiping Elohim, but from that point on, elements of Elohim became incorporated into the worship of Yahweh. The people did not want to give up their old god for a new one, and so they would worship Elohim under the name of Yahweh, and many of the attributes of Elohim became the attributes of Yahweh, including the attributes of being The Most High God.

Moses went on to lead the Hebrew people after they left Egypt under the protection, guidance, and promise from Yahweh to give them a place that became known as the Promised Land. As we know, the Promised Land turned out to be Canaan, and somewhere between Canaan and Egypt, the two gods Yahweh and Elohim merged into each other and became one and the same god known as Yahweh. Once Yahweh became synonymous with the god Elohim, the pantheon of the Canaanite gods was replaced with the doctrine of monotheism handed down to the people from Yahweh by way of Moses and the Ten Commandments.

From the time Moses led the people out of Egypt and came down from Mount Sinai with the commandments, monotheism has never stopped growing. It may have taken root with Abraham, but under Moses, monotheism flourished and became one of the most dominant features of the Ten Commandments, "Thou Shalt Have No Other God."

Try to realize that before Moses came along, whenever you went to a different area, people had their own god. There were some cities that worshiped the same god, what we call major deities, but for the most part, every civilization on earth had developed their own god. No matter how large or small the group of people was, they had come up with their own god who probably created the universe, and in all of these places, from a small village to a large civilization, we can assume they worshiped more than one god.

Yakou used to tell people he believed there was a conspiracy among the gods to make us believe in the existence of only one Supreme Being (which we call Yahweh or Jehovah) who has power over everything but allows terrible things to happen when he has the power to prevent it from happening. Yakou believed there was a god in charge of every different city who answered to a god in charge of the state that city was in. And in every city, there was a demigod in charge of every neighborhood and a lesser demigod in charge of every block, a spirit in charge of every household, all the way down to what is called a guardian angel that everyone is supposed to have.

Yakou used to enjoy smoking weed and listening to recordings of a black radical group known as "The Last Poets." His favorite song, or poem, by them was on an LP called The Fire Next Time; there is a poem on the album called "The White Man's Got A God Complex." Yakou was known throughout the neighborhood for playing this recording as loud as his stereo component could blast the sound of it. People walking past his apartment could not help but smell the unsavory odor of marijuana smoke coming from his domain while at the same time hearing the recording being played, which ended with the words repeating over and over, "I'm god, I'm god, I'm god, I'm god…spelled backward is dog."

Yakou would recite the poem word for word, and you could often hear him reciting the part, "I'm god, I'm god, I'm god…spelled backward is dog." One day, Yakou went to the park, the same park where all the dope pushers used to hang out and sell dope. At high noon, he took off all his clothes and stood in the middle of the park, stark naked, and began to yell as loud as he could.

"Kiss my ass,

I want everybody tha kiss my ass.

That's why I ain't got no clothes on, so y'all can kiss my ass.

And I want everybody tha kiss my ass.

I'm God.

That's why I want everybody tha kiss my ass, because I'm God.

God wants everybody tha kiss his ass.

That's why I want all of y'all tha kiss my ass, because I'm God.

I have the power that makes you believe anything I want you to believe.

I'll make you believe I created the universe and everything in it.

I'll make you believe my mother was a virgin, or your mother was a virgin, or somebody's mother was a virgin.

I'll make you believe I have complete control of the people running the government,

Or I'll make you believe the people running the government have no control over it.

I'll make you believe the government is completely against me.

Or I'll make you believe the people running the government only care about how much power they can get from it.

I'll make you get down on your hands and knees and bow down to me five times a day.

Or I'll make you get down on your hands and knees and pray to me without ceasing for hours and hours.

I'm God, Motherfucker.

Don't you know me by now?

I'm that voice inside your head.

I'm the one who told your father not to pull out of your mother, 'cause if he had pulled it out, you wouldn't be here.

I'm God, Motherfucker.

Don't you know me by now?"

When Yakou took off all his clothes and stood in the middle of the park proclaiming he was god, the dope pushers in the park knew the police were coming as soon as he took his clothes off, so they moved to a perimeter at the outermost boundary of the park. That way, if someone showed up who wanted to buy drugs, they wouldn't lose a customer.

And just as the dope pushers predicted, the police showed up. The senior citizens were outraged at the sight of a nude Black man standing in the park, proclaiming he was God. While they covered their eyes so they didn't have to look at him, the children in the park did just the opposite. They laughed and giggled, pointing fingers at Yakou in his nudity in a way that made it clear they wanted everyone to see.

The police took Yakou away, and no one ever saw him again..

Grandfather and Star Trek

Grandfather did not believe in using the Lord's name in vain. According to Grandfather, to use the word "Goddamn" was a sin because you were asking God to damn something. So he never used the word "Goddamn." He would always say "Got Damn" instead of "Goddamn" whenever he became angry, and that's important because the words "Got Damn" and "Goddamn" sound very much alike, but in reality, they are two different words with two different meanings. We all know what the word "Goddamn" means, but the word "Got Damn" is a word that means something has "Got Damned." As in, "a niggah gotdamned for being born black in white America" when the police said he fits the description. A junkie Got Damn for getting hooked on dope when nothing is easier to get than heroin, and people are OD-ing in record numbers. A prostitute Got Damn when her pimp beat her ass for not making enough money, or a John beat her ass because she didn't have a pimp to protect her. The word "Got Damn" clearly means that someone or something has "Gotten Damn." In the story I'm about to tell, it's important to know the difference between the two words.

Grandfather was a Trekkie. He never went to a Star Trek convention or got together with other people who loved to watch Star Trek, but he used to watch reruns of Star Trek on television. Every evening at six p.m., he'd sit on the sofa and watch another episode. According to Grandmother, he'd seen every episode ever shown on television, but he still liked to watch the reruns and see them over and over again.

One day, a rerun came on that he'd never seen before; he couldn't understand it at first because he thought he'd seen every one of them. You could imagine his joy in being able to watch an episode he'd never seen before. As the story unfolds, he realized it was an episode shown in two parts. He'd seen part one of the episode when it first aired on television, when they first started showing reruns, but he never got to see part two. This was the episode he'd missed and always wanted to see. On the night part two of the episode was shown, he'd gone to an event Grandmother wanted him to attend. It was a church concert, and Grandmother sang in the choir. While he was getting dressed, he realized it was time for Star Trek to come on TV, but he didn't have time to watch it. As he and Grandmother were on their way out the door, he looked at the darkened television set with no picture on its screen and thought to himself, "Star Trek is on right now, but I can't watch it because I gotta go to this doggone concert. I guess I'll find out what happens at the end of the television season when they show it again."

Grandfather always wanted to know what happened in the second part of the episode, and now he was going to find out. On that evening, Grandmother had gone to visit a friend who was sick, so Grandfather was home all alone. The Star Trek episodes last one hour if you count the commercials as well as the actual time of the episode being shown. The reruns have a tendency to show more commercials, especially during the last part of the program. If Grandfather had to go to the bathroom, he was always able to hold it until a commercial came on so he wouldn't miss anything. Then he'd run to the bathroom, and sometimes you could hear him yell as he would urinate in a sigh of relief. He watched the episode until it was almost over, with the whole thing leading up to a big finale. But just as he was about to find out how the story ended, the doorbell rang. At first, he tried to ignore it, but after the doorbell rang, there came a knock at the door. He thought about answering the door and getting rid of whoever it was, probably some salesman, he thought to himself, but he figured he'd wait until the last minute before he answered the door. There were less than ten minutes left to go in the program before the episode ended when a commercial came on television. At the same time the commercial came on the television, the doorbell rang again. It was as if whoever was at the door could hear the television set and knew someone was inside watching it. Grandfather figured he'd answer the door and get rid of whoever it was while the commercial was on.

When this particular rerun of the Star Trek episode was shown on television, it was during the early summer, a time of year when the sun does not go down until late in the evening. After the sun goes down, there is still enough daylight for kids to continue playing baseball or soccer till after eight-thirty p.m. Because of the extra hours of daylight, a pair of Born Again Christians were out working overtime, doing the Lord's work by going house to house, door to door, trying to save as many souls as they could. Earlier in the day, these two women had been quite successful at spreading the word of God when they came upon a person whose soul was lost in the abyss of alcoholism. They listened to him patiently for almost an hour. By the time they finished talking to him, the poor man burst into tears and swore he would never get drunk again; he was going to quit drinking and go back to AA meetings.

The two Born Again Christians were proud of themselves for helping to put an alcoholic on the road to recovery. They'd done a good day's work spreading the gospel, and by the time they came to Grandfather's door, they were feeling pretty good about themselves. When Grandfather opened the door, he was in a hurry to send them on their way and get back to watching Star Trek on television. The two ladies stood there, each holding a magazine across their chest with a big smile on their faces.

"We've come to bring you the good news," said one of them. "Did you know Jesus loves you and died to set you free?"

"Yes," said Grandfather, "I know Jesus died to save me, but I really don't have time to talk about it right now."

"We could come back tomorrow; what would be a good time for us to talk to you tomorrow?"

"Right now, it doesn't matter. I'm really busy at the moment. Just come back tomorrow."

"Well, let us leave you some of our literature about the only begotten son of God, whom the Virgin Mary gave birth to, who became our redeemer, and we believe walked amongst us as God in the flesh for a while as a human being."

When the woman said that, Grandfather could feel his blood begin to rise. He did not believe Jesus was "God in the flesh," and he didn't believe Mary was a virgin. The one who was doing the talking handed him a few pamphlets with a picture of Jesus holding a baby lamb on the cover. Grandfather refused to accept the pamphlets. He gave the Born Again Christians a harsh look and said, "Jesus and God are two different things. Jesus was not God in the flesh."

The older woman interrupted Grandfather and said, "No, but God made Jesus the only intercessor, or rather a high priest, to intercede between mankind and God." She pulled out her Bible, opened it to a particular page, and said, "If you read the beginning of the book of John, it says, 'In the beginning was the Word, and the Word was with God, and the Word was God.' Then, in verse ten of the same chapter, it says, 'He was in the world, and the world was made by Him, and the world knew Him not.' Verse fourteen goes on to say, 'And the Word was made flesh and dwelt among us.' So according to verse one, 'In the beginning was the Word, and the Word was God.' Verse fourteen says, 'And the Word was made flesh and dwelt among us,' then verse ten goes on to say, 'He was in the world and the world was made by Him, and the world knew Him not.' This is talking about God walking the earth as Jesus."

Grandfather shook his head in disagreement. "The book of John you're referring to was not written by the Apostle John, as most people believe, but was written by a group of scribes who wrote things under the name of the Apostle John around 96 AD. Absolutely nothing in the New Testament was written by any of Jesus' disciples. And as for the Apostle Paul, Paul didn't become an apostle until after Jesus was dead, so Paul never met Jesus, and he doesn't count as an apostle who was a disciple because the twelve apostles were all with Jesus when he was alive. Paul was not with Jesus when he was alive. Not one page of the New Testament was written by Jesus or any of the twelve Apostles. The book of Matthew was not written by the Apostle Matthew. The book of Mark was supposed to have been written by someone who wrote down what Peter told him to write. However, the Mark attributed to writing the book of Mark did not come along until the second century, long after Peter was dead. In fact, both the books of Matthew and Luke are based on the book of Mark and were written after the book of Mark was written. Luke, who was a physician and companion of Paul, did not write the book of Luke, so the whole New Testament is nothing but hearsay, based on what someone else told someone else about Jesus long after he was dead."

Grandfather paused for a moment to catch his breath, and just as the woman started to speak, he cut her off and started talking again. "And as for the Virgin Mary, Jesus was the firstborn son of the Virgin Mary, and in the book of Matthew, Jesus has four brothers and at least two sisters. There's this part in the Bible where Jesus is preaching a sermon, and the Virgin Mary shows up along with her other children, who are Jesus' brothers and sisters. Jesus doesn't stop preaching to say hello to them, and someone in the crowd asks Jesus, 'Aren't you going to say hello to your mother or brothers and sisters?' Jesus answers back, 'She that does the work of the Lord, she is my mother, she is my sister, he that does the work of the Lord, he is my brother.' So, the Virgin Mary gave birth to more than just one child. The New Testament gives the names of four boys the Virgin Mary gave birth to other than Jesus, and it says He had sisters, not a sister but sisters, which means the Virgin Mary gave birth to more than one girl. So, the Virgin Mary gave birth to at least seven children before she died, but only the first one she gave birth to was the Son of God."

Grandfather paused for a moment as if he was giving her a chance to speak. The woman got ready to say something, but before she could say a word, Grandfather started talking again.

"If the Virgin Mary was not a virgin when she died, I don't think she was a virgin when Jesus was born. Why would God choose a woman to be the mother of his child if, afterward, she was going to have at least six other children by someone else, who was a mere mortal human being named Joseph? And we don't know for sure if Joseph, her husband, was the father of all of her other six children because Joseph died before Jesus was crucified. When Jesus got crucified, there was this other Joseph who went to Pilate and asked for the body of Jesus so they could bury him. But let's get back to Joseph, the husband of Mary—everyone knows that Mary's husband, Joseph, was not the father of Jesus. People see Mary and Joseph as being the same age, but my research shows that Joseph was most likely much older than Mary. Back in those days, women didn't have rights like they do today and did not get to choose who they would marry; they were told who they would marry. So more than likely, the marriage between Joseph and Mary was an arranged marriage between an older man and a younger woman. Speaking of the older men in the Virgin Mary's life, has it ever occurred to you that Zacharias, the father of John the Baptist, might also be the biological father of Jesus Christ?" Grandfather paused, making it clear he was allowing her to answer his question.

The woman told Grandfather she wasn't interested in his theories about Zacharias being the father of Jesus and wanted to get back to the subject of Jesus being the only child of the Virgin Mary. She said, "The writers of the New Testament used the Aramaic idiom when writing it. In that sense, certain people were not brothers and sisters, even though the literal translation implies it. The people mentioned in the New Testament as Jesus' brothers and sisters were probably his cousins; at any rate, they were the people he grew up with and were as close to him as his family; that's why the New Testament refers to them as his brothers and sisters. The Virgin Mary only gave birth to one child, and that was Jesus."

Grandfather disagreed, saying, "The New Testament says he had brothers and sisters, and you're telling me they were not his brothers and sisters because of the way you chose to use Aramaic? You're going to stand there and tell me what was written in the New Testament means something different than what it says just because it was written in Aramaic?"

Grandfather told the woman he never lost his faith in God, but there were some parts about Jesus he didn't believe in.

"Jesus said some wonderful things, and I believe in just about everything Jesus said, but what Jesus said and what Jesus did are two different things to believe in. I don't believe he walked on water or rose from the dead; I believe he died on the cross when that Roman soldier stuck a spear into his side and killed him, and I don't believe Jesus was the biological son of God." By now, Grandfather realized he'd said more than he'd intended to say and went back to trying to get rid of them. "Like I said, I'm busy at the moment and don't have time to talk about it."

"Well, let us give you some of our literature about the good news," said the woman.

"Okay," said Grandfather, hoping they would hurry up and leave if he accepted the pamphlets they were passing out.

"If you're interested in continuing the conversation tomorrow, what would be a good time for us to drop by?"

"About one o'clock," said Grandfather. "My wife will be here tomorrow, and she'll be glad to talk to you about Jesus. Bye-bye, have a good day." And with that, Grandfather closed the door as they were saying goodbye.

As soon as Grandfather closed the front door, he turned around to look at the television set. He saw the names of the actors as the credits rolled across the screen right before it went off the air. The Star Trek episode ended while he was talking to the Born Again Christians. Grandfather became angry and yelled out loud, "Goddamn Born Again Christians."

The two women were still standing on the front porch. It had only been a few seconds after Grandfather closed the door when they heard him yell "Goddamn Born Again Christians." The two ladies left and did not come back at one o'clock the next day or any other day.

Notwithstanding: This was a word I came across and didn't understand, so I asked Grandfather what the word meant. Grandfather rubbed his chin, and I could tell by the look on his face that he was thinking hard about what the word meant. After a short while, he looked at me and said, "The word 'not' means to don't do something. We all know what the word 'not' means, and the word 'withstand' means to be able to stand up to something, like the house could not withstand the storm and it caved in, or Muhammad Ali could not withstand Joe Frazier's punches and lost the fight. So, when we put the two words together, it means 'not to withstand something.'"

Uncle Junior was in the room when I asked Grandfather what the word notwithstanding meant. Uncle Junior was Grandfather's oldest son, and he was the first person in the family who ever went to college. Uncle Junior called me over to him and said, "In spite of what I'm about to say, and notwithstanding what your Grandfather just told you, it would behoove you to get a dictionary and look the word up."

"Behove?" I yelled out. "What the—" (I wanted to say what the hell does behoove mean but caught myself from saying hell). "What does behoove mean?" I asked.

Uncle Junior replied, "You might as well get used to looking up words in the dictionary if you're going to go to college when you get older. By the time you get through college, the dictionary will be your best friend." He told me to get him a piece of paper and something to write with. I found him a pencil and a piece of paper. He wrote down both words and told me, "These are how the words are spelled. Now it's up to you to look them up."

Virginity - Shot To Hell

As children, we used to look up to just about all of the adults. We had this one aunt we used to love to hang around, who was my favorite. She was always happy to see us, and one of the things I remember the most about her was the way she talked to us children. She would kneel, squat, or bend over to look us in the eye when she talked to us, whereas other adults would stand tall and straight, towering over us, and look down at us for eye-to-eye contact. If she knew you had a lot to say, she would always find a chair to sit in when you talked to her so you were looking at her at eye level. For some reason, the other adults seemed to consider her to be at the lower level of the pecking order.

One day, my sister, Mary Jane, overheard some of the adults talking about our aunt Esther. One of them said her virginity was shot to hell, and Mary Jane wondered what her virginity was and why someone would shoot it. So, she asked Grandfather about it and wanted him to explain to her what virginity was and why someone would want to shoot it. Grandfather took a deep breath, sat back in his rocking chair, looked at Mary Jane, and said, "Give me a minute to think about it." After a while, he told Mary Jane she was too young to understand what virginity is, but it was something spiritual, something very valuable, more precious than silver or gold, something that existed inside her in a very special part of her body.

Some day, she would grow up and get married, but before she got married, she would know all about virginity and how important it was for her to give her virginity to the right man. He told her, "When you grow up, you're supposed to give your virginity to the man you marry, and you're supposed to give it to him after you marry him, not before you get married. Some girls get confused about that and give it to the man they want to marry before they marry him. But either way, once you give your virginity away, it's gone for life, and you can never get it back. Now, the person you give your virginity to is gonna have it for the rest of his life. That's why it's important to give your virginity to the man you're going to marry after you've married him because he's the person you're going to be with for the rest of your life, just like your grandmother and I are going to be together for the rest of our lives. If you give your virginity to a man before he marries you, and after you've given him your virginity, he decides not to marry you, there's nothing you can do about it. For the rest of your life, he'll have your virginity, and when the man you're going to marry comes along, you won't be able to give him your virginity because somebody else has got it. You and your husband will have to spend the rest of your lives together without your virginity, and when you get old and you're about to die, you'll want to know if the person you gave your virginity to went to heaven or hell. Because wherever he went, your virginity went with him. If the person you gave your virginity to went to heaven, then your virginity went to heaven and will be there waiting for you when you get to heaven, but if the person you gave your virginity to went to hell, then that's where your virginity will end up. And that's why your aunt Esther's virginity is all shot to hell, because the person she gave it to got shot and went to hell."

Right about that time, Grandmother walked into the room. She told us children to go outside and play because she wanted to talk to Grandfather, and she didn't want us around because what they had to talk about was grown folks' conversation. We ran outside and pretended like we were playing, and while some of us were actually playing, the rest of us ran up to the front porch as quietly as possible and got underneath the window on the front porch. From there, we could poke our heads up enough to listen through the window to hear what they were saying.

"Umm, umm, umm," said Grandmother, looking at Grandfather. "You ought to be ashamed of yourself." Grandfather looked back at her with a puzzled look upon his face and said, "What?" As if to ask, what did I do now? Grandmother said, "I heard what you said to Mary Jane, and you know doggone well Leroy didn't get shot and go to hell. Leroy's the person Esther gave her virginity to as far as we know, and he's still alive."

"Well, I had to tell her something," said Grandfather. "And I sure couldn't tell her the truth, that her aunt Esther's a junkie who's hooked on heroin and the person she gave her virginity to is the one who got her hooked on it."

"Just because Leroy's a junkie doesn't mean he's going to hell," said Grandmother. "It's not too late for him to straighten up."

"That boy is not about to straighten up as long as he's shooting that crap in his arm. Once he stops using it, he can begin to straighten up, but until then, he might as well be shot to hell."

"Leroy ain't dead yet; where there's life, there's hope. He can always pull himself back up and make a new man of himself."

"Yeah, and Jesse Jackson can unite forces with the Black Muslims and try to form our own government, but we both know that ain't gonna happen. And Leroy ain't gonna quit shooting heroin."

"Well, at least he's alive, and that means Esther's virginity isn't shot to hell because he's got it, right?"

Grandfather looked at the floor and became quiet, like he knew the answer but didn't want to say it.

Grandmother spoke up again, saying, "If he's not shot to hell, Esther's virginity is not shot to hell, right?"

Grandfather looked at Grandmother and said, "Leroy ain't got Esther's virginity; he gave it to somebody else."

"Say what?" exclaimed Grandmother.

Grandfather went on to explain, "The first time a man gets sodomized, he loses his virginity in a different way from the way he loses it the first time he has sex with a woman. If Leroy got sodomized after Esther gave him her virginity, whoever sodomized

Leroy got Esther's virginity while he was sodomizing Leroy," said Grandfather.

"You don't actually believe that, do you?" Grandmother asked him.

"Listen," said Grandfather, "Leroy and Esther will sell their bodies to whoever will give them the money for them to buy some dope. Spanky, the cab driver, was down at the barber shop telling everybody about Leroy getting sodomized by a homosexual named Luther. According to Spanky, Leroy was pimping Esther and was trying to get a businessman named Luther to pay him to have sex with her when Luther told Leroy he liked having sex with men more than he liked having sex with women. Luther offered Leroy fifty dollars if he would give him a blow job and let him sodomize him. And you know he and Esther both can get high for days on fifty dollars' worth of dope. So Leroy and Luther hopped in a yellow cab, and Spanky was the cab driver. He took 'em to the No Tell Motel, and according to Spanky, they were feeling each other up in the back seat before they got there. He said you could have sex with Esther if you bought her a ten-dollar bag of heroin or maybe a five-dollar bag if you caught her when she needed a fix, and the same thing applied to Leroy. Any man who wanted to have sex with Leroy would find him more than willing to have sex with another man for twenty dollars if he didn't need a fix. If he needed a fix, the price was a lot cheaper, and Leroy was much more willing to do things he wouldn't normally do for twenty dollars."

"So, about that time, I said to Spanky, 'You sure seem to know a lot about Leroy having sex with other men. How do you know so much about what Leroy will do and won't do for twenty dollars?'"

He says, "Man, I'm a cab driver; you'd be surprised at what goes on in the back seat of a taxi cab after midnight. A lot of prostitutes use taxi cabs at night, and people don't have time for a motel or they're too damn cheap to pay for one, so they slip me a five-dollar bill, and I look the other way. About half the cab drivers who work the night shifts make deals with prostitutes to get paid two or three dollars to look the other way while the prostitute gives the john a blow job in the back of their cab. And in just about every case, it's the John, not the prostitute, who pays the cab driver, so I want five dollars or else find another cab. After all, it's the John who's paying, not the prostitute, and once she causes him to get an erection, he won't mind paying the five dollars compared to what a motel will charge 'em. It's a known fact that prostitutes are known to use the back seat of a taxi cab as a place of business."

"I'll say one thing for Luther: he ain't cheap. He spent fifty dollars on Leroy, plus the cost of the motel, because what Luther wanted to do, they couldn't do in the back of a cab. And after Luther took Leroy to the No Tell Motel, Leroy's been in the back of taxi cabs at night giving blow jobs to men like he enjoys doing it. Then, during the day, he and Esther shoot up all the money they make at night. He may have started out pimping Esther or trying to pimp Esther, but right now, he himself has become a male prostitute, and it won't be long before he'll be wearing a dress, and someone will be pimping both him and Esther."

Grandmother replied by saying, "You don't fool me, Geary. I know you all too well. You said Leroy didn't have Esther's virginity because he got sodomized, and when I asked if you actually believed Leroy didn't have Esther's virginity because he'd gotten sodomized, you avoided the subject and started telling a long story about Spanky driving his taxi to the No Tell Motel. So explain to me once and for all how someone could get Esther's virginity away from Leroy by sodomizing him."

"It's hard to put it into words," said Grandfather, "but remember when I was telling Mary Jane that her virginity was a spiritual thing?"

"Yeah, I remember," said Grandmother.

"Well, it's kind of like this: when a woman gives a man her virginity, he gets something spiritual from her at the same time while he's getting her virginity. If a man is a virgin and has never had sex with a woman, there's a spiritual transference that takes place the first time he has sex with a woman, and the woman gets something spiritual from the man even if the woman isn't a virgin. But when a man gets sodomized, he loses his virginity in a different way. Everybody has a spirit, and every human being has a certain amount of spiritual power. When a man gets sodomized by another man, he loses his spiritual power to the person who sodomizes him while he's being sodomized."

"What if it's a woman who gets sodomized?" asked Grandmother.

"The same thing applies to her. Whatever spiritual power she has will go to the man who sodomizes her," said Grandfather.

"What if it's not a man but another woman using one of those things made of latex? Does she get her spiritual power?" asked Grandmother.

"Now you're asking me something I don't know for sure. I would imagine she would need to have a real penis, not one made of latex, in order to get another woman's spiritual power by sodomizing her. I'm sure there are ways for one woman to get another woman's spiritual powers by having sex with her, but I have no idea how one woman gets another woman's spiritual powers by having sex with her. I only know I believe it's possible."

"But you do believe it's possible for a person's virginity to go from one person to another even though they only gave it to one person to begin with?" asked Grandmother.

"Well," said Grandfather, "I suppose I do."

"And you believe it's true?"

"Of course, I believe it's true. If it wasn't true, I wouldn't believe it," said Grandfather.

At this point, Grandmother sat down on the sofa in the living room. Up until now, she'd been standing while she was talking to Grandfather, but once she sat down, the whole tone of their conversation seemed to change. She looked at Grandfather with a look on her face that Grandfather recognized as an I've got you now kind of look. There was a smile on her face similar to the one in the painting called the Mona Lisa. She looked at Grandfather and said, "What about the Virgin Mary?"

An expression came across Grandfather's face that changed his demeanor; Grandmother knew how he felt about the subject, she knew which buttons to push and not to push, and as soon as she said "The Virgin Mary," Grandfather's defense mechanisms kicked in. In the language of Star Trek, Grandfather's shields went up.

"What about the Virgin Mary?" said Grandfather.

"You just said if it wasn't true, you wouldn't believe it. People believe The Virgin Mary lived her whole life and died a virgin. Just because they believe it doesn't make it true."

Grandmother was about to say something when Aunt Esther came bursting into the room.

She looked at Grandmother and said, "Mama, I know I owe y'all money, but right now, I need help. Leroy's in jail, and I've gotta get him out."

Before Esther could say anything else, Grandfather cut her off in the middle of what she was saying.

"NO, Hell no. We ain't giving you no money to get that nigga out of jail. And don't even think about asking us to put up our house as bail money."

"But Daddy, we gotta get him out," cried Esther.

"We ain't got to do nothing. He got himself in jail, and he can get himself out," said Grandfather.

"That's just it. He can't get himself out. It has to be somebody on the outside who ain't in jail that gets him out."

"Listen," said Grandfather, "if Leroy stays in jail long enough, he'll get cleaned up while he's in there. Jail is a good place for him to kick the habit. He can't get no heroin while he's in jail, and if you don't get him out right away, he'll be much better for it when he does get out."

Esther burst into tears, then looked at Grandmother and said, "Momma, please don't turn your back on me, please, Momma, please help me get Leroy out of jail."

"Baby, we ain't got the money to give you, and you know your father ain't about to put up this house and take a chance on losing it to get Leroy out of jail."

"Yeah, Mama, I know," said Esther, "but we gotta do something. If we don't get him out, nobody will, and if he stays in jail, he'll get killed or sent to the hospital from being beaten so badly by them other inmates. You know, there are a lot of people looking for Leroy who wanted to hurt him that are in jail. People who said they were gonna kill him if they ever caught up with him for ripping them off. And Mama, Leroy would always act as a go-between for people who wanted some dope but didn't have the connection. He'd take their money, and they'd never see him again. He stole a lot of things from a lot of people. And jail is full of the people that Leroy has stolen things from."

"Please, don't remind me what Leroy took from me and your father," said Grandmother. "Listen, the church is known for helping people when they need help. Why don't you go talk to the Reverend and ask him for help? Maybe the church can find a way to get Leroy out of jail."

"Oh, Mama, the church ain't gonna do nothing. I haven't seen the Reverend in years; it's been ages since I've been to church. And Leroy won't go near a church, you know the church only helps its members for something like this. If I was hungry, the church might give me some food. It might help me find a place to stay and give me some clothes to put on my back, and if I was sick, they might get me some medicine, but for getting someone out of jail, the church ain't getting no one out unless he's a member of their church and a member in good standing, like a deacon or an usher. In order to get Leroy out of jail, the church would have to put up the bail money. And you know how the church is about money. It's alright for them to ask me, you, and everybody else for money, but what's gonna happen if I ask the church for money, the money to get Leroy out of jail?"

"Well, I go to church every Sunday, and I consider myself to be a member in good standing. Let's find out what'll happen if we ask the church to put up the bail money to get Leroy out of jail. Let's go talk to the Reverend and find out if they'll help get Leroy out of jail."

Esther suddenly became excited. "Mama, if you go with me, they might just get him out."

About that time, Grandfather spoke up and asked, "Exactly what did Leroy get arrested for this time?"

Esther said, "Leroy was in the park, you know, that park where all the dope pushers hang out, and he was talking to Booker, asking him if he could front him a dime bag until Wednesday of next week when, all of a sudden, police cars came driving into the park from every direction. As soon as Booker saw the police coming, he took off running. Booker must have had about a hundred dollars in dime bags of dope on him when the police cars drove into the park, and he didn't want to get caught with any dope on him, so he started emptying his pockets and throwing the dime bags onto the ground as he took off running. Leroy took off right behind him and was following him, running right behind him, picking up every dime bag Booker threw away while he was trying to get away from the police. So Leroy got arrested for possession of every dime bag Booker threw on the ground. And now the police want Leroy to testify against Booker to say that Booker was selling drugs in the community."

"But Booker was selling drugs in the community!" said Grandfather.

"That ain't the point," said Esther. "If we don't get Leroy out of jail, the other inmates will kill him to keep him from testifying against Booker."

"Over a hundred dollars worth of heroin," said Grandfather.

"He's in jail," said Esther. "First of all, a hundred dollars in jail ain't like a hundred dollars on the street. A hundred dollars is worth a lot more in jail than it is on the streets. Second of all, you ain't never been in jail, so you wouldn't know what it's like. Leroy is being forced by the police to testify against Booker, and if he doesn't testify against Booker, he'll go to prison for a felony conviction. Plus, the police can always get inmates to beat him up in order to testify against Booker. And the dope pushers don't care what happens to him as long as he keeps his mouth shut and doesn't say anything against Booker."

"No, no, no," said Grandfather. "If he keeps his mouth shut, the dope pushers shouldn't be worried about him, but you're right about him going to prison for a few years."

Grandmother told Esther, "Come here," and motioned for Esther to sit beside her on the sofa. Esther crossed the room to where she was and sat down beside her. Grandmother gently reached out, took Esther's hand, and said, "The first thing tomorrow morning, we'll go down to the church and talk to Reverend Johnson, and if he and the church don't get him out of jail, we'll find some other way to get him out."

Esther became happy at the realization that her mother was going to help her get Leroy out of jail. "Oh, Momma, the reverend might do it if you asked him. I'm sure the church would support you if you asked them for help."

"Then that settles it," said Grandmother. "Tomorrow morning, we'll contact Reverend Johnson and see if the church will help us get Leroy out of jail." Esther grabbed Grandmother and gave her a hug. For a moment, the two of them just hugged each other as if nothing else mattered.

The next day, Esther arrived bright and early. Grandmother let her in and insisted she have breakfast before they left the house. Esther took a seat at the dining table, and Grandmother went to the stove, heating up the frying pan. Grandmother took a few strips of bacon out of the refrigerator and waited for the frying pan to get hot before putting the bacon in. "You know," she said to Esther, "breakfast is the most important meal of the day. We've already eaten, and before you and I go anywhere, I want to make sure you've had a good breakfast. Once we leave the house, there's no telling what's gonna happen or how long it'll take to find a way to get him out, and if you don't have a good breakfast by the time noon gets here, your stomach will think your throat has been cut." Grandmother set an empty coffee cup in front of Esther and poured her a cup of coffee. Esther took a few teaspoons of sugar from the sugar bowl on the table, added some to her coffee, then stirred and took a sip. "Ah, that's good," she said. "Coffee in the morning sure does hit the spot."

Esther suddenly changed her demeanor, became very sarcastic, and in as serious a voice as she could manage, said, "I love the smell of caffeine in the morning; smells like victory." She and Grandmother both started to laugh. It was an inside joke based on a movie they'd seen called Apocalypse Now. After watching the movie, "I love the smell of caffeine in the morning" became a regular saying at the breakfast table. Esther reached into her purse, pulled out a pack of cigarettes, and after taking one out, asked if it was okay if she smoked. By now, the frying pan was hot, and the sound of bacon sizzling as it landed in the pan marked the unmistakable beginning of breakfast being prepared.

"No," said Grandmother, "I don't mind. I quit smoking years ago, but I can still remember what it's like to have that first cigarette with a cup of coffee in the morning, or any cigarette with a cup of coffee."

Esther lit her cigarette, then took a draw off of it and inhaled deeply. She seemed to relax as she exhaled the smoke; her head went back, and she blew a column of smoke into the empty space above her. By now, Grandmother was beating pancake batter in a mixing bowl, getting ready to pour it onto the grill as soon as the bacon was done. Esther knew how much her mother enjoyed cooking for other people, especially her children, and for a brief moment, Esther felt like she was home again. Her mother was fixing her breakfast like she had done for what seemed like over a thousand years, and Esther could feel the bond between them as mother and daughter, a bond that had existed before she started elementary school.

As soon as the bacon was done, Grandmother placed it in the oven to keep warm, cleaned the grill, then poured four circles of pancake batter onto it. After that, she cracked two eggs, emptied them into the skillet, and in no time, breakfast was done. A few minutes later, Grandmother sat a plate of hot food in front of Esther with a smile on her face that showed how happy she was to watch one of her children eating and enjoying the meal she had prepared for them. Esther put out the cigarette she'd been smoking, then looked at the meal her mother had set before her and said, "Talk about a grand slam breakfast." She dove into the pancakes before eating anything else on her plate. Pancakes were her favorite breakfast food, and Grandmother knew it. She washed the pancakes down with a large sip of coffee. She looked at Grandmother and said, "Momma, you always did make the best pancakes I ever ate. Aunt Jemima ain't got nothing on you."

By now, Grandmother had sat down at the table across from Esther and was pouring herself a cup of coffee.

"Do you remember when you were a little girl, and your father and I took you, your brothers, and your sisters to see a movie called Imitation of Life?" Grandmother asked Esther.

Esther shook her head yes while still eating and uttered the sound "um-hum," as if to say yes.

"I always thought that movie was about the real Aunt Jemima," said Grandmother. "I was never able to find out for sure if it was just made up or if it was about the real Aunt Jemima, but everyone I know who's seen the movie swears it's about the real Aunt Jemima."

Esther stopped eating and said, "If I live to be a hundred, I'll never forget the part where Aunt Jemima dies, and her daughter comes running up to her mother's coffin crying and saying how sorry she was. I cried my eyes out when I saw that."

"So did I the first time I saw it. Your father took me to the theater to see it when it first came out. Back in those days, a movie would play at a movie theater in one city, then it would play in a different city at a different movie theater after it left the first city, and it would go from city to city and state to state. After about a year or two, it would come back to the city you saw it in if it was a good movie. Gone with the Wind, The Ten Commandments, and Ben Hur were all movies that played in movie theaters year after year after year, and it was like that with the movie Imitation of Life. Every year, your father and I would go see that movie when it came around until we got tired of seeing it. Then they made the remake with Lana Turner, and we had to see it, but one thing we did was make sure our children got to see that movie. Even if it ain't about the real Aunt Jemima, it's one of the most beautiful movies ever made about race relations in the United States."

Grandmother took a sip of her coffee, and for a while, the two of them just sat there without saying anything—Grandmother drinking her coffee while Esther wolfed down the breakfast Grandmother had made her.

After Esther finished eating, she looked at Grandmother and said, "Thanks for fixing me that breakfast, Mama. It really hit the spot."

Grandmother told Esther, "Today is a weekday, so Reverend Johnson should be easier to get in touch with. I happen to know he's busier on the weekends than he is during the week. But he's out there seven days a week doing the work of the Lord. I think it's best if I call him first and let him know we're coming to see him." Grandmother got on the phone and called his number. After a few rings, someone answered the phone.

Reverend Johnson was the same Junior Johnson who grew up with Grandfather. He'd taken over his father's church, and Grandmother never stopped going to the same church even if Grandfather no longer went.

"Hello," said the voice at the other end of the line.

Grandmother spoke into the phone, "Hello, may I speak with Reverend Johnson? This is Eleanor, Eleanor McAlister. What's that? The reverend ain't in? Well, when will he be back? Oh, I see.

We'd like to make an appointment to see him as soon as possible. Um-huh, this afternoon sounds fine. Ok, we'll be there at one o'clock." Grandmother hung up the phone and looked at Esther, who'd been sitting there the whole time and heard everything Grandmother said over the phone. Esther spoke up and said, "So we're gonna see him this afternoon at one o'clock?" Grandmother shook her head yes and said, "He's not there right now, but when he does get back, he'll be expecting us at one o'clock."

Esther told Grandmother she'd be back at twelve noon, and they would have plenty of time to get there. But first, she had some important things to do.

Grandmother tried her best to make a smile come over her face as she looked at Esther. She knew that Esther was going to go get her a fix between now and one o'clock. Esther had shot up that morning before she left her hotel room, but it was just enough to keep the monkey off her back. By one o'clock, she knew she'd be needing a fix—one more powerful than the fix she had that morning. The fix she had that morning was enough to give the impression she was sober. The fix she planned to have at one o'clock was one that would make her sit back or lie down because she would not be walking around talking to people after she got high. Esther had planned to finish talking to the reverend and be back at her hotel long before noon. So now Esther had to reschedule her day around how she was going to shoot up. She could not slip into a nod while talking to the reverend, and she didn't want that monkey on her back either. She would work things out so that by twelve o'clock, she would not need to shoot up for a couple of hours. She was not a morning person. She was used to staying up late in the evenings and not getting out of bed until eleven o'clock or around noon. Esther went back to her hotel and finished shooting up the amount of heroin she originally wanted to shoot up that morning.

Esther arrived back at Grandmother's house just before twelve-thirty. She knew it would take them twenty minutes to get to the church, so they still had plenty of time to get there. Esther was not wearing any sunglasses when she came to see Grandmother that morning, but when she returned about twelve-thirty, she had on a pair of dark sunglasses. Grandmother was sure she knew the reason why, but nevertheless, it was a sunny day, and although it was a warm sunny day, the fact that Esther was wearing sunglasses was a sign she was high. Esther seemed to walk slower than a normal person would walk. After taking so many steps, she seemed to stop and pause in an attempt to reestablish her balance before she took another step. They got into Grandmother's car and drove to the church where Reverend Johnson would be expecting them.

It was clear Esther was high, and if Esther were to be totally honest, she would admit to shooting up more heroin than she intended to use. Grandmother could tell from her demeanor she was high—her movements, the way she talked, and the sunglasses.

Esther was constantly looking down, not looking into Grandmother's face when she spoke to her like she'd done earlier that day. They didn't talk much during the drive over to the church, not like they had talked at breakfast that morning. Esther fiddled with the car radio, changing the stations until she found her favorite station, and they listened to the music. "Say it Loud, I'm Black and I'm Proud" was a song playing on the radio.

"God," said Esther, "I can't believe what that song has done for the black race of people in America. Before James Brown made that recording, we were calling ourselves Negroes, and a lot of us didn't want to identify with the black people in Africa."

"I know what you mean," said Grandmother. "A lot of us thought we were more sophisticated, more educated than the black people in Africa. We were colored people, which meant people of color, or we were Negroes, but we weren't black until James Brown came out with that song. From that time on, we no longer called ourselves Negroes or colored people. It was as if overnight we identified with black people in Africa or black people all over the world for that matter."

It wasn't long before they arrived at the church. They walked into the building, which was the church Grandmother had been a member of for most of her life. Esther stood beside Grandmother as they walked inside the church she used to go to when she was a little girl. Once inside the church, she came to a complete stop, then grabbed Grandmother by the arm and squeezed it. Esther took off her sunglasses and just stood there looking up at the high ceiling with its huge wooden rafters. Her head slowly looked around at the stained glass windows in the white plastered walls as if she were taking it all in. Grandmother wondered what Esther was thinking. She knew Esther hadn't been in that building since she was a teenager. She could tell from the way Esther grabbed and squeezed her arm that Esther was having a soul-stirring experience. Something deep in her soul was being touched by God.

Grandmother used to watch the World News every night, and there was a phrase journalists used that she hated. A week wouldn't go by without some journalist on the national news saying the phrase "An Existential Moment." Local newscasters didn't seem to say it as much, whereas national newscasters found it one of their favorite expressions. She and Grandfather would watch the news every night, and they both did not like it when the newscaster would describe something taking place or an event that had taken place as "An Existential Moment," as if time stood still for a brief moment, or as if this was the moment when the course of history would be forever changed. This was the defining moment in time. Grandmother and Grandfather looked up each of the words in the dictionary, and they decided that every moment in time is an existential moment, according to the dictionary. But now, Grandmother felt like what she was experiencing was a real existential moment in her own private world when she looked at Esther and saw how she seemed to be momentarily lost in the melancholy moments of her past, catching up with her future, and leaving her stranded in the present. Esther remembered one of the sermons Reverend Johnson preached when she used to sing in the choir. The sermon was about having an impure thought.

Reverend Johnson once said, "There are passages in the Bible where it talks about having a clean house. Imagine you had gone grocery shopping and came home with a carload of grocery bags. You start to unload the bags of groceries from the car and bring them into your house. There are so many grocery bags that you prop the front door wide open and leave it open until you can get all of the groceries out of the car and into your house. After you get all of the groceries into your house, you close the front door, and soon afterward, a small rodent runs across the floor alongside the base of the wall. It darts under the sofa or behind the refrigerator, stove, or any place where it can hide. You realize, while you were busy getting groceries out of the car, it was able to get into the house while the front door was open. As soon as you see it, you go get mouse traps or poisons or whatever it takes to get rid of it. If you can afford it, you may even call the exterminator. Well, having an impure thought is much like having a rodent in your house. Ya see, God wants all of your thoughts to be pure, and how can you be pure if your thoughts are impure? Now, in the metaphor I just used, there's a big difference if the rodent is a mouse or a rat because a rat is much larger than a mouse, and a rat can do far greater damage than a mouse. It takes a much larger trap to catch a rat than it takes to catch a mouse. The same thing applies to having impure thoughts."

Esther thought about what she'd gone through since she had left the church, how many impure thoughts ran through her mind on a daily basis—bigger than the largest rat anyone had ever seen. She wondered what Reverend Johnson would think of her if he knew she had been working as a prostitute and was a heroin addict.

The churches did not have a vestibule. When a person walked into the church, the first thing they would notice was the high ceiling and an altar straight in front of them at the end of the aisle on the opposite end of the building. There was a wide aisle with wooden pews on each side of the aisle in front of them. At the end of the aisle was a huge wooden cross in the back of where the reverend would sit. The wall was covered with extravagant curtains hung on golden curtain rings. The curtains were the exact same color as the carpet on the floor—red. The chair in which the reverend sat was similar to a throne made out of wood that had a high, elongated back to it, which faced the congregation. Beside his chair were smaller chairs on either side that his deacons and guest preachers sat in, also made out of wood, and they seemed to look like smaller thrones for they were larger than any normal-sized chairs but smaller than the chair the reverend sat in. There was a podium in front of the chair where the reverend stood. Everything on the altar was elevated, and when the reverend got ready to speak at the podium, he had to step down to it because the podium was on a lower level than where he sat, but still elevated, as it was part of the altar. This was done intentionally, for there were times when someone else other than the reverend would speak at the podium while the reverend sat in his presider's chair, which was directly behind the podium, giving the distinct impression he was in full support of the person who spoke at the podium. Add to that, everyone in the back of the podium was on a higher level than the person speaking at the podium, which caused the persons behind the podium to be slightly looking down at whoever was speaking while the audience was looking up at them. The choir section was catty-corner against the far walls of the church, and the whole outward appearance of the church seemed to focus on the reverend's chair—a real cathedra that looked like a throne. Even when the chair was empty, it expressed a symbol of the throne of God. When a person walked in the door, the reverend's office was near the entrance of the church, off to the side after you walked inside. In a way, it was so the reverend could ambush a person from their flank before they were expecting to see him. When a person came into the building, they would be looking at the high ceiling and the altar straight in front of them.

Esther took a deep breath, then looked at Grandmother and shook her head yes as if to say she was alright. Esther's high had started to come down, and she was sure it was being in church that brought her high down. About that time, the door opened to the reverend's office, and Reverend Johnson stepped out. He'd heard the sound of the front door opening and closing, and he knew someone had entered the church. He was expecting Grandmother and Esther to show up about that time and came out of his office to greet them.

"Hello, Reverend," said Grandmother with a wide, sincere smile on her face. She was always happy to see him.

"Hi, Reverend," said Esther. She was also smiling, but the smile on her face was much different than the one on Grandmother's face. The smile on Esther's face was one of embarrassment. The Reverend exchanged greetings and invited them into his office while he held the door open.

Grandmother and Esther went through the open door the Reverend was holding open for them and walked past the secretary's outer office into his office, then had a seat. The Reverend followed them into his office, closing the door behind him. He then sat down behind his desk and asked, "What can I do for you?"

Grandmother explained to the Reverend how Leroy was in jail, and they were hoping the church could help them get him out.

The Reverend listened patiently to everything they had to say, then told them there was very little he could do. The church was not going to put up the money they needed to post his bail. He said, "What Leroy needs is an attorney. The church has a relationship with some attorneys, and if we can get one to take on his case pro bono, the attorney should be able to get him out." The Reverend looked through his Rolodex, stopped, and copied down a name and phone number on a piece of paper. He gave it to Grandmother and said, "Have Esther call this number and talk to this man who's an attorney. Tell him I gave you his number and told you to ask if he could help you. Esther should be the one to call him because she's the one trying to get him out." Grandmother took the piece of paper he had written on and handed it to Esther. She took it and held it in her hand, looking at it and feeling as if it was what they had come for. Once Leroy got out of jail, he would still have to go to court and stand trial. If Leroy could get an attorney to fight his case, he would have a much better chance of winning than with a public defender. Esther looked up at the Reverend with a huge smile on her face and thanked the Reverend for giving it to her.

Grandmother was happy to get any kind of help that he could give her. But she couldn't help noticing the way he looked at Esther. It was as if he wanted to smile at Esther but didn't want them to see him smiling at her. The Reverend wished them the best of luck and then politely found the words to get rid of them as soon as he could. Grandmother loved to talk to the Reverend about anything, seeing as he was one of her favorite people to talk to. She was not one of those people who talked a lot, but talking to the Reverend was different from talking to anyone else she knew. Once she got started, it was like she could see the spirit of the Lord inside the Reverend, and it caused something inside her to stir until she found herself talking in a cathartic release of feelings and emotions. The Reverend knew she would talk his ear off if he had the time to listen to her, so he explained how he had other appointments and people expecting to see him.

Grandmother and Esther left the church feeling good. The high Esther was feeling when she left the church was a natural high compared to the kind of high she had when they arrived. When they got back to Grandmother's house, Esther called the attorney on the phone. His receptionist answered, and after being put on hold for a short while, the attorney spoke to her, saying hello and politely asking, "How are you doing today?"

Esther became excited at the sound of his voice asking her how she was doing; his showing concern assured her he would help Leroy.

"I'm not doing too well," Esther replied. "My boy…" Esther was about to say "my boyfriend" but caught herself and said "my fiancé." "My fiancé is in jail, and I'm afraid people in jail are going to kill him if I don't get him out soon. He's made a lot of enemies, and most of them are in jail. It's just a matter of time before they get to him."

The attorney on the other end of the phone spoke up, saying, "My name is Robert Perkins. Reverend Johnson contacted me a little while ago and said you'd be calling me, so I was expecting to hear from you. I'm going to be pretty busy the rest of the day. Is there any way you could meet me downtown after five o'clock? I have to finish up the day with a client at the Cecil Hotel on Main Street. We could meet in the lobby about 5:30 or 6 o'clock. If the hotel has a restaurant or a bar, I could meet you there if you prefer."

Esther knew where the Cecil Hotel was and said she'd meet him in the lobby at 5:30. He replied, "I'll see you then." After he said that, she hung up the phone. The Cecil Hotel was two blocks south of 7th and Broadway. There were a number of buses that ran past 7th and Broadway, seeing how Broadway was more of a main street where most of the local buses ended up going down. She could catch any one of them that ran down Broadway, get off at 7th, walk down two blocks, and be there within an hour from the time she got on the bus, or she could catch whichever bus ran down Main Street and get off at 7th. But it would take her much longer than an hour to get there.

Esther took the bus that ran down Broadway. She got off at 7th and Broadway and walked two blocks to the Cecil Hotel. It was a little before five o'clock when she got there, so she went into the cocktail lounge to have a drink in order to kill time and calm her nerves before meeting the lawyer she hoped would get Leroy out of jail. Like most bars and cocktail lounges, the lights were low, and there were no windows, so if a person came in off the street during the daylight, it would take several minutes for their eyes to adjust to the darkness of the dimly lit room.

The clock was about to turn five o'clock, which meant it was Happy Hour, and anyone with a job who was an alcoholic or on their way to becoming an alcoholic would end up in a bar as soon as they got off of work. Esther ordered a drink, then took her drink from the bar and sat in one of the empty booths. She felt comfortable sitting there alone in the darkness, having a booth all to herself.

People getting off work were filing into the bar, and Esther was sure if she stayed at the bar by herself, someone would try to pick her up and engage her in conversation when she didn't want to be bothered. As she sat there, she thought about a place on Santa Barbara Avenue off of Crenshaw, in an area known as Crenshaw Square. This was a place where pimps and prostitutes used to hang out, a very popular spot. During the day, it was a regular bar, but at night, it was one of the hippest nightclubs in town. She and Leroy were regulars there, and she was known to turn tricks at this nightclub, and Leroy was known as her pimp.

There were plenty of nightclubs in Los Angeles where prostitutes went to find clients, but this was a Black nightclub where Black people were accepted for who they were. It was owned and operated by Black people, and every so often, a major league athlete who was Black would show up and hang out with everyone there, which made the place extremely popular. Every Black person who did not have enough money wanted to go there. Every Black person who had enough money did go there, even if they didn't like the place—they had to go there to see what it was about. Esther sat there reminiscing about the time she and Leroy used to watch the entertainer Rudy Ray Moore perform at the nightclub, and she wondered how the nightclub ended up with the name "Blueberry Hill."

At exactly 5:29, she walked out of the cocktail lounge and into the main lobby of the hotel. She just stood there looking around, wondering how she would know which person in the lobby was the lawyer she came to meet. She hadn't stood there too long before a man came up to her and asked, "Are you Esther McAlister?"

Esther found herself looking into the eyes of a nice-looking Black man who was at least ten to fifteen years older than herself.

She replied, "Yes, I'm Esther McAlister."

The man spoke up and said, "I'm Robert Perkins. I spoke to you over the phone."

Esther could not help but think the man had a nice-looking face and attractive build.

"Is there someplace we could sit down and talk?" he asked. There were end tables and chairs in the lobby of the hotel, but for some reason, Esther felt more comfortable going back to the cocktail lounge she had just come out of. Once there, they could sit at a booth and have much more privacy, so they both went into the cocktail lounge and sat in a booth across from one another.

Robert Perkins smiled at her and said, "Reverend Johnson told me some of what happened, but I need to hear from you exactly what happened and what you want or need me to do."

Esther told him the story of how Leroy got arrested and went on to explain that her greatest fear was what would happen to Leroy if she didn't get him out of jail as soon as possible. Robert Perkins told her the cost of an attorney was expensive, but he would be willing to work as Leroy's attorney in exchange for her services in a way that was nothing new to her. He knew she worked as a prostitute, and Leroy was her pimp. He told her there was someone who wanted to have sex with her, and if she agreed to have sex with him, this person would pay her attorney fees.

Esther sat there in the dim light of the cocktail lounge. She reached into her purse, pulled out a pack of cigarettes, and lit one. She took a long draw off the cigarette and let it out. It didn't take her long to realize she could not afford an attorney, and she had become accustomed to selling her body to pay for the drugs she and Leroy used, so she agreed to the deal Robert Perkins was offering.

Robert Perkins had made reservations for a room in the hotel before she had arrived. If Esther said no, he would cancel the reservation. He told Esther he had already gotten a hotel room, and the person who wanted to have sex with her was waiting in the room. He asked her to think of this person as her benefactor, someone who had seen her from afar when she was at the nightclub called Blueberry Hill.

At Blueberry Hill, there would always be a line of girls that she would somehow be standing in. Most of them were prostitutes, some were models or aspiring actresses, and the person who wanted to be her benefactor always thought she was the prettiest one standing in line.

Esther was an attractive woman. She had a beautiful face and a slender body. She did not eat much, which kept her stomach muscles tight and flat. Esther was not a small woman, but her measurements were well proportioned. She was about average height, average breast size, but the part of her body she was most proud of was her ass. She was self-conscious about her ass growing up, so she did an extensive amount of squatting exercises until her ass was just the right size, and she loved to dance. She would dance until she worked up a sweat, with beads of perspiration dripping from her body.

Dancing, to her, was more than just an exercise that kept her in shape. It was something sacred, as if she were in contact with a higher power that was able to cause her body to move in an eloquent manner. Leroy used to say she had the most beautiful ass he'd ever seen. He took one look at her ass and fell in love with her. It had a perfectly round shape, perched on top of two muscular thighs with beautiful legs underneath them.

When she and Robert Perkins left the cocktail lounge, he found himself staring at her ass as she stood in front of him after sliding out of the booth they were sitting in. He found it difficult not to look at her ass and could not stop checking her out as they made their way out of the cocktail lounge, across the lobby, and into the elevator.

Once the elevator doors closed, there was a silence that made everything seem awkward. Esther's heart was pounding, and she wondered who was waiting for her in the hotel room they were going to. Robert Perkins didn't say a word; his eyes looked straight ahead at the lighted numbers over the elevator doors, but he was thinking about what Esther's body would look like without clothes on, and every so often, his eyes would drift in her direction until her frame came into view.

Finally, the elevator stopped at the third floor, and the doors opened. What was only three floors seemed like an extremely long time for an elevator to get there. They both stepped out of the elevator and began to walk down the hall. Robert Perkins pointed to the hotel room they were going to. As they approached the room, he took the key from his pocket, stuck it into the lock, and before opening the door, he looked at Esther and said, "When I open the door, you won't see anyone in this hotel room waiting for you to come inside. I'm the one who wants to have sex with you."

He then turned the key and opened the door to the room. The room was empty. Esther looked him in the eyes and could tell by the way he looked at her that he wanted her. So you're gonna be my benefactor, Esther thought to herself as she looked at him and smiled.

The room had a queen-size bed, end tables on each side of the bed with matching table lamps, a small desk to write letters on, and a television. There was also a small armchair in the room, positioned where a person sitting in the chair would be looking directly at the bed.

Robert Perkins came close to Esther, gently put his arms around her waist, and pulled her body close to him. Then he started to kiss her while simultaneously caressing her hips, thighs, and buttocks. His hands went up her back and unhooked the back of her dress. He started to remove her clothing in a manner that made it clear he wanted to get her undressed as quickly as possible but did not want to seem anxious for her to become naked.

Up until now, Esther's main concern was doing what she had to do to get Leroy out of jail, but now her instincts as a hustler were beginning to take over. This man was a lawyer, and everyone knows lawyers make a lot of money. Earlier, he'd mentioned being her benefactor, which to her meant having sex on a regular basis. She put her hand on the side of his face and kissed him back, letting her tongue slip inside his mouth. Then she started to unbutton his shirt. He finished unbuttoning her dress and pulled it down over her shoulders, letting her dress fall to the floor.

Esther rubbed his chest and stomach muscles. She could feel his heartbeat as he took off his coat, tie, shirt, and undershirt. She unbuckled his belt, unbuttoned his pants, and slid her hand down below his waist until she could feel his penis. She began stroking his penis with one hand while running the other hand inside the groove that separates the buttocks. It didn't take long for him to get an erection.

As soon as he got an erection, Esther stopped stroking his penis and took off her bra and panties while he took off his underwear. They were both naked. Once again, Esther reached down, took his penis in her hand, and slowly began to stroke it. She looked him deep in the eyes and said, "Before we do anything, there's something I need to know. Earlier, you talked about being my benefactor, so I need to know right now before we have sex if this is gonna be a one-night stand or are we gonna do this on a regular basis?"

Robert Perkins said, "I'm gonna be honest with you, this whole thing is a business arrangement, and you will get paid, but there is someone else who wants to have sex with you, only he wants me to have sex with you first, and if you won't have sex with me he doesn't think you'll have sex with him. I'm about ten years older than you, and he's older than I am. I don't know how many times we'll have sex, but I do know he's your regular basis when it comes to having sex."

He then slid his hand between her thighs and began to fondle her vagina, and asked, "Is that okay with you?"

Esther could feel his fingers moving around inside her as he played with her clitoris. They began to kiss one another passionately and fell on top of the bed. He seemed to end up on top of her in what is known as the missionary style.

"Come on, baby, come on, baby," Esther would say to him as she moved her entire body in conjunction with his membrane inside her, "Come on baby, that's it, give it to me, give me what you got, I want you to get all I have to give to you, so you come back for more."

They were at it hot and heavy. Robert Perkins was going full throttle and was in a position known as "up for the down stroke" when there was a knock on the door. The knock was three rapid knocks that came very quickly. The knocks seem to come from inside the hotel room, not the door that a person used to go in and out of the room from the hallway outside. Robert Perkins recognized the knocks as a signal and knew he had to act quickly. As soon as he came down from his upstroke, he grabbed Esther around her waist and flung her and himself over one hundred and eighty degrees so that he was laying on his back and she was on top of him.

When Esther heard the three knocks, she knew it came from inside the hotel room. She began to speak out in a loud voice and said, "Hey, wait a minute, I hear someone in here with us. What's going on?" But all she had time to say was "Hey" before Robert Perkins flipped her over, and she found herself laying on her stomach with Robert Perkins underneath her.

As soon as Robert Perkins flipped her over, the closet door opened. Someone had been in the closet the whole time, and Robert Perkins knew it. Before the two of them left the cocktail lounge, the benefactor had already gotten a key, went up to the room, and was hiding in the closet before they got there. Once they started having sex, the benefactor cracked the closet door open and was looking at their two bodies, trying to become one.

As he watched them commit an act of procreation without any intention of trying to procreate, he began to masturbate while looking at them. When he felt himself almost ready to reach his climax, he knocked on the closet door three times as a sign to Robert Perkins that he was coming out of the closet. Once Robert Perkins was on his back with Esther on top of him, the benefactor came out of the closet, climbed on top of Esther, and stuck his penis in Esther's anus while Robert Perkins restrained her. As soon as he got his penis all the way inside her anus, he began having an orgasm. Esther felt him as he stuck his penis inside her rear end; she could feel his penis throbbing inside her as he ejaculated.

He began to shout out loud as he reached his climax in her anus,

"Ahhhhhh."

He was laying on top of her when he yelled as a result of reaching his climax. It was as if he yelled directly into her ear, and she recognized his voice.

"Reverend Johnson," exclaimed Esther with a tone of surprise in her voice. "Is that you, Reverend Johnson?"

"It's me, baby doll, it's me," said Reverend Johnson. He ran his hands from her thighs up to her breasts and back down again. "Baby doll, baby doll, you are my baby doll," said Reverend Johnson. "I've been in love with you since you were a young girl. I've known you since before you were born. I watched you grow up, and I remember when your mother brought you to church every Sunday after your father quit going. I remember when you sang in the youth choir right before you started to go through puberty, and years later, just before you were supposed to become a member of the senior choir, something happened that caused you to stop going to church when you were about fifteen years old. A few years later, I heard you'd been turned out and were being pimped by your boyfriend—the man you're trying to get out of jail."

Reverend Johnson shifted his position, then slid off of her body so that he now lay next to her on the bed and continued to talk to her. "You must have been seventeen or eighteen when you started turning tricks. If I'm right, you're twenty-five years old, and your pimp, the man you're trying to get out of jail, is somewhere in his early thirties."

Esther interrupted him, saying, "He's more than just my pimp. He's my fiancé, and we're engaged to be married."

Reverend Johnson said, "I know you love him, baby doll. There ain't a person on earth who loves that man more than you do. Look at what you're doing right now to get him out of jail."

At about this time, Robert Perkins got out of bed, went to his coat laying on the floor, took out a pack of menthol cigarettes and a lighter, then got back in bed and lit up a cigarette. The three of them lay naked on the bed, passing the one cigarette back and forth until they each ended up lighting up and smoking their own.

Robert Perkins still had an erection. As he lay there on his back, he reached over, took Esther's hand, and put it on his penis. Then he slid his hand across her stomach down to her vagina and started playing with her clitoris.

All three of them were lying on their backs, smoking cigarettes as if they were all on a cigarette break.

Robert Perkins and Esther fondled each other with one hand while smoking a cigarette with the other. Neither one of them had reached their climax, and without saying a word to each other, they both knew what was on the other's mind because they were thinking the same thing. Reverend Johnson was not on the same page. He'd just finished having his climax and was now daydreaming about Esther's place in his life in the near future while he enjoyed the menthol of the cigarette he smoked.

Reverend Johnson began to talk, or rather, it was like he was having a daydream out loud.

"The first thing we'll do is get you into a program that will get you off drugs. Then we'll get you into college. You're still pretty young, not too old to go to college. While you're in college, I'll take care of everything you need—rent, food, clothing, and anything else you need. All you have to do is go to college and get a degree. If you don't believe me, ask Robert. I took care of him from the time he was in high school until he passed the bar and became a lawyer, and after that, I helped get him a job with a law firm. Go ahead. Ask him."

Up until now, Esther had been stroking Robert's penis and thinking about having an orgasm, but now she stopped, turned her head to the side, looked at him, and asked if it were true.

Robert turned his head to the side to look at her and said, "What he's talking about is a scholarship. I've known the reverend since I was a boy. My parents brought me into his church long before you showed up. By the time you sang in the church choir, I'd finished college and was in law school. The reverend made it all possible. He was the one who signed the papers that gave me the scholarship that paid for everything I needed to become an attorney. Anything I needed that wasn't included in the scholarship, the reverend took care of just by signing his name on a grant, a fellowship, or what have you. He wants you to go to college. I don't know what plans he has for you after that, but believe me, the reverend is a person who can pull strings for you. That scholarship I was talking about, I would never have gotten it without his signature on the document."

Going to college was the last thing on Esther's mind. She had dropped out of school when she was sixteen years old, gotten pregnant by Leroy, and had a miscarriage. From the time she had the miscarriage, she made sure never to become pregnant again and had gotten sterilized. She was used to a life in the fast lanes. College was not in her plans and didn't fit into her lifestyle. She had thought about getting into a program that would get her off drugs and had planned to do it in a couple of years, but not right now. She was not about to quit using drugs today, tomorrow, or the next day.

As she lay on the bed, she realized the Reverend was her benefactor, not Leroy's, and it didn't take long to figure out the Reverend wanted her in his life but did not want Leroy in her life. She turned her head to face the Reverend, who was lying on the other side of her, and said, "I know you have plans for me in your life as my benefactor, but what about Leroy? He's my fiancé, and it sounds like you don't have any plans for him in my life, or you don't want him in my life."

The Reverend got out of bed and walked over to where Robert Perkins' pants lay on the floor. He picked up his pants, retrieved the wallet, and took out one hundred dollars. He put the wallet back in the pants and walked back to the bed. Robert Perkins said nothing and did not seem bothered that the Reverend took one hundred dollars out of his wallet without asking for permission. He just lay there caressing the thighs of Esther's body.

The Reverend walked over to the bed, handed Esther the one hundred dollars, and said, "Here's a hundred dollars. I want to see you make love to Robert right now. You're gonna get paid for what we're doing tonight, but this is a little extra. I wanna see you and Robert get down."

Esther looked at the hundred dollars he gave her. Her purse was lying on top of the end table. She got out of bed, put the hundred dollars in her purse, then got back in bed and curled up next to the attorney, Robert Perkins.

The Reverend sat in the chair facing the bed. Esther looked at him and wondered, had the chair been placed in that position in advance, or was it just a coincidence that the chair gave him a perfect view of her and Robert on the bed? The Reverend wanted to watch, and the way he sat in the armchair convinced her everything was planned in advance. The Reverend was into voyeurism; he was one of those people who liked to watch other people having sex.

Esther began to kiss Robert on his chest and slowly made her way down to his genitals, where she performed an act of fellatio on him, making sure the Reverend got a good view of his penis going in and out of her mouth.

The Reverend began playing with himself as he watched Esther give Robert a blowjob.

Without warning, Esther stopped sucking his dick, quickly climbed on top of him, and stuck his penis into her vagina, all in one smooth motion as if she'd done it a thousand times. She made sure the Reverend had a bird's eye view of Robert's penis going inside of her vagina.

The reverend was the same age as Esther's father, who was sixty-five years old, and at sixty-five years old, he suffered from premature ejaculation. It did not take him long to have an orgasm; in fact, there were times when he started to ejaculate while he was trying to insert his penis inside the person he was attempting to have sex with. Once he had his orgasm, he had to wait a good while before he could get another erection. The reverend remembered what it was like to be young. The thing he missed the most was the way his penis would stay hard as long as he wanted it to; that added to the fact that his penis would not get nearly as hard as it used to when he was young and after the first orgasm he could have another orgasm in five to ten minutes.

The reverend was now looking at a close-up of Esther's ass going up and down with Robert's penis underneath her, going in and out of her vagina. The reverend could feel himself beginning to have an orgasm and stopped masturbating. He wanted it to last a little longer so he could enjoy playing with himself some more, but the train had left the station, and there was no stopping it from arriving at its destination.

The reverend was breathing hard as he started to ejaculate. He felt an orgasm, although not as powerful as the first one he felt when he sodomized Esther, and he wished he could have made it last longer. The reverend sat there with semen in his lap. After a few minutes, he got up and went into the bathroom to get a towel to wipe himself off. When he came out of the restroom, he saw Esther and Robert going at it; they were bucking like a pair of wild stallions, and he knew he could never satisfy her the way Robert was satisfying her.

But the worst part was, Robert wasn't trying to satisfy her; he was trying to satisfy himself. As the reverend looked at them both, trying to satisfy themselves, he thought to himself, I came out of the closet too early, I should have waited until now to sodomize her. He remembered another occasion when he was masturbating while waiting in the closet. As soon as he came out of the closet, he started to ejaculate. By the time he reached the bed, he had finished having his orgasm. He climbed on the bed and tried to sodomize the person, but he did not have an erection. No matter how hard he tried, he could not penetrate the person he was trying to sodomize. He felt humiliated, and it pained him to think about it. It was something he swore he would never let it happen again.

The reverend reached in the closet, got his clothes out, and proceeded to get dressed while Robert and Esther continued to get each other off. The whole time he was getting dressed, he couldn't take his eyes off of them. Once he got dressed, he sat down in the arm chair and watched them having sex until they both had finished reaching their climax. The reverend then got up out of his chair and walked over to the night stand near the head of the bed where Esther's purse was.

He then laid three one-hundred-dollar bills on top of Esther's purse and said, "I have to go now, but Robert will keep in touch with you and let you know when we'll meet again. If you need anything, you contact Robert, and Robert will get in touch with me. I want you to go through Robert to get in touch with me. No one knows anything about this. I can afford to stain my clothes, but I cannot afford to stain my reputation. If you tell anyone about our arrangement, I'll deny it, and you will never get a red cent out of me for the rest of your life. But if you keep our agreement, if you keep me satisfied in a sexual manner, I'll look after you the same way I looked after Robert when he was coming up. Robert can tell you anything you need to know about what's expected of you. He'll contact you and let you know when I want to see you again." After he said that, the reverend left the room.

Esther lay on the bed and looked at the hundred-dollar bills on top of her purse. She realized the reverend never answered her question when she asked him if he wanted Leroy in her life. However, when the reverend put one hundred dollars in her hand, her instincts took over, and they told her to get the money. Leroy would still be there after she got the money. Anytime there's an opportunity to get some money, you've got to get it while you can because it won't be available for long.

Esther reached across the bed and picked up the one-hundred-dollar bills to look at them. She lay on her back and held the bills in the air over her face. Then she seemed to examine each one as if she was checking to see if they were counterfeit. For her, it was a force of habit. She knew the reverend was not the kind of man to pay someone with a counterfeit one-hundred-dollar bill. She also knew that when people accept counterfeit hundred-dollar bills, they don't know the money they're accepting is counterfeit. So when they go to spend it, usually they'll give it to someone else, and the counterfeit bill goes from one hand to another until someone with a keen eye examines it, or it gets taken to the bank, where the bank will know it's a counterfeit bill.

As Esther lay on the bed examining the bills, Robert, lying next to her, began to speak to her.

"I don't think you know how powerful the reverend is. After Dr. Martin Luther King Jr. became the face of the civil rights movement, he formed a network of black preachers all across the United States. This network of black preachers in the civil rights movement had been going on before the Montgomery Bus Boycott, but when Martin Luther King Jr. came along, the network exploded. Black preachers all across the country lined up in support of Martin Luther King Jr., and Reverend Johnson was one of them.

When Martin Luther King gave his 'I Have a Dream' speech in Washington, D.C., at the Lincoln Memorial, Reverend Johnson was there at the protest. He was one of the preachers who met with Dr. King on more than one occasion. Although he was not a close friend of the man, he can honestly say he knew Dr. Martin Luther King Jr., and so can every other preacher who is a part of the network because Dr. King made it a point to personally meet with each of the black preachers that were supporting him.

Now, don't get me wrong when I say the network of Black preachers who supported Dr. Martin were all black preachers. There were white preachers as well, and there were Catholic priests, Jewish rabbis, and white Protestant preachers who marched with Dr. King. They are all a part of the network of preachers that supported Dr. King, and even though Dr. King is dead, that network of preachers that he met with still exists today.

Martin Luther King Jr. is one of the greatest martyrs of our time. He and John F. Kennedy, and the network of black preachers that he put together, plan to make him the greatest martyr of all time, even greater than John F. Kennedy. The greater the martyr Dr. King becomes, the greater the influence of his disciples and the people who knew him. The reverend is very much involved in the civil rights movement, and as someone who went to his church, I'm sure you know it. So, if you want to get on his good side, other than having sex with him and satisfying him sexually, you'll get out there and do something that involves civil rights. There are protests and demonstrations you could show up at, and there you'll meet people that will help you join an organization fighting for civil rights."

"Let me be as blunt as possible: the reverend is your sugar daddy, and as your sugar daddy, there are certain things required of you as his sugar baby, or baby girl, doll, or whatever you want to call it. The first and most important thing is not to let anyone know you're having sex with him unless it's someone he wants to know you're having sex with. Take Leroy, for instance. When Leroy gets out of jail, he's going to have to realize that the reverend comes first. Although Leroy may see himself as your pimp, he's gonna have to see how the reverend has plans for you that don't include him. The reverend will allow you to continue to see Leroy as long as he doesn't get in the way. But when Leroy gets out, he's not gonna be telling you who to have sex with. Either he finds someone else to pimp, or his pimping days are over."

Esther had stuffed the hundred-dollar bills in her purse while he talked. She'd been in love with Leroy since she was sixteen or seventeen years old. Her family did not approve of Leroy and always claimed he was the one who got her hooked on dope. Esther's uncle used to say Leroy used black magic to cast a spell on Esther, which caused her to fall in love with him. Esther always thought that particular uncle was crazy, as did the rest of the family, but they seemed to agree with him on why Esther fell in love with Leroy. For her, the reason why she fell in love with Leroy could be summed up in a song by Aretha Franklin called Dr. Feelgood. In the very last part of the song, Aretha Franklin explains exactly why she loves Leroy more than she has ever loved any man in her life. The last line of the song goes, "Good God almighty, the man sure makes me feel real good."

Esther spoke up and said, "So exactly what does the reverend want me to do other than have sex with him?"

Robert answered her, "For one thing, he wants you to get off the drug heroin; he mentioned you going to college after you get clean and sober. I'm sure he'll want you to go to college and get a degree, but he won't expect you to go to school until after you've quit using heroin."

Going to school was the last thing on Esther's mind. She was used to living the street life. Her world consisted of hustlers, players, and pimps. There was an invisible line the reverend wanted her to cross that was more like an invisible wall. On one side of the line were the people who obeyed the law; on the other side of the line were the people who had little respect for the law and found themselves disobeying it whenever the opportunity arose.

When the reverend gave her a hundred dollars or when he put three hundred dollars on top of her purse, he didn't see himself as breaking the law, but Esther did. It's been called the oldest profession known to man, and just because they make a law against it doesn't make it wrong. People have been paying other people to have sex since civilization began, and people will be doing it until the end of time, no matter how many laws they make against it.

When the Reverend Johnson came out of the closet and Robert perkins restrained her while the Reverend sodomized her, what they did was tantamount to an act of rape, but Esther didn't see it as rape as long as she got paid she just saw it as doing business.

Esther did not feel like she was doing anything wrong by accepting money in exchange for sex. Obviously, the reverend and Robert Perkins felt the same way. When it came to her heroin addiction, she could see why it was wrong and why there were laws against it, but she felt it was her physical body, and she had the right to do whatever she wanted to do with her physical body as long as it didn't interfere with anyone else.

She spoke to Robert Perkins and said, "I've thought about getting clean and sober from time to time, and I plan on doing it someday, but not now. I'm just not ready to quit right now."

"You'll never be ready to quit," said Robert. "Until something so terrible happens that makes you wish you had quit using long ago, something so bad it makes you feel like life is no longer worth living because the grief you're feeling is just too unbearable. Then you'll quit, because the pain you feel from your withdrawal when you quit using will act as a counterweight to the grief you've been feeling. But by then, it'll be too late, because you'll have already lost something or someone whose loss will forever create a vacuum in your life that is irreplaceable. There will be a hole in your soul that will create an emptiness inside you that you'll never be able to fill, and you'll never be able to stop trying to fill that void that comes from doing drugs over a long period of time.

"Whether you know it or not, the reverend is trying to save you from the self-destruction you're headed toward. To say he wants to help you is an understatement. He wants to make you a part of his life, and you have to realize what it takes, what sacrifices you have to make, in order to fit into his life and exactly where you fit into his life. One thing I can tell you for sure, if you're willing to make those sacrifices and try to give up drugs and go back to school, your future will be much brighter than the future you have now with Leroy."

When he said the name Leroy, Esther jumped at the opportunity to ask about how Leroy would fit into her life. "Speaking of Leroy," Esther exclaimed, "exactly how does the reverend feel about me and Leroy? He knows Leroy and I will be living together after he gets out of jail."

"As long as you agree to do whatever the reverend asks you to do, he'll take care of you. If you and Leroy want to live together, that's something you have to get okayed by the reverend. He's gonna be paying your rent, so he might not want Leroy living with you. But I need to know right now. Are you going to go along with the program? Because if you're not going to do what the reverend wants you to do, he's not gonna be your sugar daddy."

Esther gave him the most sincere look she could muster and said, "I honestly don't know if I can, but I'm willing to try. Getting off drugs is not gonna be easy, and if I'm able to get clean and sober, going to college is a lot harder than kickin' heroin, but I know the reverend wants me to have a better life than the one I got now, and I'm willing to do whatever he asks."

"That's good enough for me," he said. "Tomorrow arrangements will be made to get you into a drug rehab program. Someone from my office will call you at the phone number you gave us to contact you, which I assume is your parent's phone number."

Esther shook her head yes. He then told her, "If you can be at your parent's house tomorrow afternoon between one and four o'clock, when the person from my office calls, you need to be there to talk to them over the phone. After that, we'll get started on putting you someplace where you can't get drugs." He reached over, grabbed one of her breasts, and started to fondle it. She, in turn, reached down, grabbed his testicles, and began to fondle them in a manner that quickly caused him to become aroused. Within a short amount of time, they were having passionate sex with one another again.

The next day, Robert Perkins went down to Los Angeles County Jail and met with Leroy. He told Leroy he would try to see if he could get him released on an "OR," which stands for own recognizance, but it was highly unlikely because of his record. He wanted Leroy to consent to go into a drug rehabilitation program in order to get him out. Robert felt more than likely the district attorney would object, and the judge would set bail from one to ten thousand dollars, but it wouldn't hurt to ask the judge if he would release Leroy on his own recognizance.

Leroy was supposed to go to court that day for his arraignment. Robert Perkins told him he would be there at his arraignment and asked if there was anything he wanted to ask him before he left. Leroy said no, and Robert Perkins told him he would see him in court at his arraignment later that day.

Esther made it a point to be at her grandmother and grandfather's house the next day by one o'clock. She'd thought long and hard about giving up heroin and what it would be like to go into a program that would help her get off drugs. She thought about Leroy, and she knew if Leroy did not get off of heroin, she would end up having to choose between the kind of life her benefactor, Reverend Junior Johnson, was willing to provide her with, or the life she would continue to have with Leroy once he got out of jail.

As she waited by the phone for it to ring, she thought about how she and Leroy couldn't afford a phone because just about all their money went into buying drugs. The one-room hotel they stayed in had a payphone in the hallway, and everyone who lived in the hotel would come out of their room and run to answer it whenever it rang because it was the phone they'd given out the number for someone to call them at.

There was a rule about the payphone: if no one was in the hallway and you were on the phone, you could talk as long as you liked, but if someone came up who wanted to use the phone while you were talking, you had to end your conversation and hang up the phone within five minutes. It was known as the five-minute rule. The hotel was filled with drug addicts and nefarious types of individuals. It was the cheapest, most rat-infested place she had ever lived in, but as long as she and Leroy were together, it didn't matter how raggedy the place they lived in was. It was a place where they could shoot heroin into their arm and not be looked down upon by their neighbor when they walked out of their hotel room.

There was a bathroom at the end of the hall, which had a shower in it, but the showers only had hot water in the mornings for the people who went to work or looked for a job. There was a huge boiler in the basement used to heat the water in the hotel, and the people who ran the place would cut the boiler off in order to save money. If you wanted to take a shower after 9 a.m., the water was lukewarm at best, but the boiler stayed off until the early morning of the next day. Although cooking was not allowed in the rooms, the vast majority of people who stayed there had a hot plate in their room from which they were able to cook their meals.

All of Esther's clothes were purchased at the Goodwill or Salvation Army thrift store, and she always dressed nice. One who never shopped at a thrift store would be amazed at the nice clothes you can get for such a cheap price. Her secret for being immaculately dressed was to go to as many different thrift stores as she could find and purchase the cream of the crop.

She and Leroy used to go to the second-hand stores together looking for clothes. They would both get all their clothes second-hand or stolen. When people see you dressed in clothes that look good, people don't care if the clothes are stolen or second-hand. People only care about the way you look, and they looked marvelous when they showed up at nightclubs and other places where they would make money as purveyors of carnal delight.

The phone rang, and suddenly Esther was drawn back into reality as if an invisible hand slapped her across the face and yelled, Wake up. She picked up the receiver and spoke into it.

"Hello," said Esther.

"Hello," said the voice of a woman on the phone. "I'm calling on behalf of Attorney Robert Perkins. Mr. Perkins has asked me to inform you that your fiancée, Leroy Jones, is being released from custody. At the present time, his release papers are being processed, but he'll be released from jail within a few hours. You should receive a phone call from him letting you know to pick him up. Mr. Perkins also asked me to give you this number to call and see about getting into a rehabilitation program. The number is 213-565-7894."

Esther said, "Hold on, let me get a pencil and paper to write it down." She went and got a pencil and paper, then asked the woman to give her the number again. Esther wrote down the number, then thanked the woman and hung up the phone. As soon as she hung up, she felt a wave of relief, knowing Leroy was going to be alright, while at the same time, the relief she felt was being replaced with a feeling of obligation that weighed upon her shoulders like a burden she could not get rid of.

The Reverend had delivered on his promises, so she owed him, but now that Leroy was out of jail, he was going to hit the streets and go back to a life of shooting drugs in his arm and doing whatever he had to do to sustain that kind of lifestyle. If I could get Leroy to give up drugs, we could live together, and the reverend would still take care of me, Esther thought to herself. But as long as Leroy's using drugs, the reverend is not gonna allow us to live together.

Esther came to the conclusion Leroy would have to give up drugs, or she would have to give up the reverend as her benefactor. The reverend was more than just a benefactor; he was someone who could open doors for her. She'd just paid her back rent this morning from the money he'd given her last night, and she still had enough left over to pay for two months' rent in advance, which she was not about to do, but it felt so good to know you had the rent money long before it was due.

She thought of Robert Perkins and what he had told her, how the reverend would pay her rent as long as she did what he wanted her to do. She did not like staying in the rundown hotel she lived in and was sure the reverend would help her get an apartment. By help, she meant he would get her an apartment and afterward help her pay the rent each month. At that moment, she came to a decision: she would explain to Leroy how she got him out of jail and tell him he had to give up drugs in order for them to be together, or she would break up with him.

Esther took the phone and dialed the number of the rehabilitation center. After a person answered the phone, she gave them her name and said she wanted to come into their program to get off drugs. An appointment was made for her to come into the center at 9 a.m. the next day, and Esther hung up the phone.

Grandmother came into the living room from the bedroom and asked if the phone call she had just heard was the call Esther had been waiting for.

Esther said yes and told her she was going into a drug rehabilitation program. That phone call she just received gave her the number to call for a program she would be going into. She said, "Leroy's getting released from jail in a few hours, and he needs someone to pick him up."

Grandmother said, "It all depends on what time he gets released. You know I have to pick your father up from work when he gets off. If Leroy gets released from jail early enough, I can pick him up first. Otherwise, he'll just have to wait till after I pick your father up from work. But I sure am glad you're going into a drug rehab program. Thank the Lord above. Is Leroy going into the rehab program with you?" she asked.

"I don't know," Esther replied. "I just know this is something I have to do if I want life to get better. When I see Leroy, I'm gonna tell him. Either he gives up drugs or gives me up, but he can't have both of us. If I'm gonna get clean and sober, he's gonna have to get clean with me. I can't do it and be with him unless he quits using drugs with me."

"You have no idea how glad I am to hear you say that," replied Grandmother. "If you're really serious about getting off drugs, you have to separate yourself from the people that are still doing drugs. Otherwise, you'll never stop using 'em."

Esther had always had a close relationship with her mother. There was no one on earth she could talk to the way she could talk to her mother. Esther looked up at Grandmother and said, "Momma, last night I had a dream. Now, there are times when my dreams are just ordinary dreams, but there are times when my dreams are real. I mean, there are times when I wake up from my dream, and I feel like everything that happened while I was dreaming is something that actually happened, even after I wake up. Well, last night, I had one of those dreams. I dreamed that I was standing on a stage in front of a thousand people, and there were other people on the stage with me, and we were dressed in caps and gowns. All of us were getting our college degrees, and in my dream, I was graduating from college. Momma, that dream was real. I know I can do it if I quit using drugs. And in the dream, you, daddy, and everyone else were in the audience cheering for me when I got my degree. And I looked around for Leroy because he was the only one missing. The more I looked around for Leroy, the more the dream began to change. Suddenly, I was somewhere else, and Leroy was telling me what I had to do in order to survive. I told Leroy no, I wasn't gonna do it, and Leroy and I got into an argument because he wanted me to do something, and I refused to do it. That's when I woke up from the dream."

"Baby, there is nothing on earth I would rather see than to see you go to college and get a college degree," said Grandmother. "But it seems clear to me your dream is telling you you're gonna have to give up Leroy in order to get your degree. Anyway, it's time for my soap opera to come on."

Before Grandmother could say another word, Esther looked her straight in the eyes and said, "General Hospital."

Grandmother exclaimed, "Yes, Lord, I got to find out what's happening with Audrey. She got raped by her husband, and a lot of people don't feel like it's rape if a husband forces his wife to have sex when she doesn't want to. The way I was raised, it was considered a wife's duty to have sex with her husband whenever he needed it, which could also be interpreted as whenever he wanted it. If a wife said no, he could always go to some other woman, and from that point on, it would be the wife's fault their marriage was in trouble. Back in the old days, a lot of women used to hate having sex with their husbands but saw it as a requirement of the institution of marriage; things are a lot different today."

Esther could see her mother beginning to go on a tirade about a woman's place in the institution of marriage and was trying to think of a way to stop her by changing the subject. She quickly interrupted her mother while she was talking and asked, "What channel does General Hospital come on?"

"It comes on Channel Seven," said grandmother.

Esther got up and walked over to the television to see what channel it was on.

"It's already on Channel Seven," said grandmother. "All of my soap operas come on Channel Seven. First is Ryan's Hope, then there's All My Children, after that is One Life to Live, and last but not least is my favorite, General Hospital. I usually do the housework while the other soaps are on TV, and I'll glance at the television set to see what's going on. But when General Hospital comes on, I sit down and give it my undivided attention."

Esther spoke up and said, "I remember we used to say, 'Ryan hopes that All My Children will have One Life to Live at General Hospital without any Dark Shadows.' Speaking of Dark Shadows, does that soap still come on TV?"

"You know I never did watch that show," replied grandmother. "The kids seem to like it, but I just never cared for it. If my memory serves me correctly, the show went off the air this past April. They replaced it with Password."

"Password?" exclaimed Esther. "They should have stuck with Dark Shadows if you ask me. I'll take Dark Shadows over Password any day of the week."

The television show General Hospital came on, causing Esther and grandmother to both become quiet as the words General Hospital flashed upon the screen of the TV set. They sat there with their eyes glued to the television set for about an hour and said very little to each other. Right after the show ended, the telephone rang. It was as if somehow the phone had waited to ring until after the TV show they were watching ended. Esther was still sitting next to the phone, so she answered it.

"Hello," she said into the phone, then she seemed to listen to whoever was talking to her. After a while, she spoke up and said, "Okay, we'll come get you. We should be there in about a half hour or so." She hung up the phone and looked at grandmother.

Before she could say anything, grandmother spoke up, saying, "That was Leroy, wasn't it?"

Esther shook her head yes and said, "He wants us to come get him."

"He's got perfect timing," said grandmother. "We should be able to pick him up and have plenty of time to pick up your father when he gets off work."

Esther spoke up and asked, "Momma, is it okay if you drop me and Leroy off at our hotel before you go to pick up daddy?"

"I don't see why not," said grandmother. "It's not that far out of the way. I can drop the two of you off and still make it in time to pick up your father."

About a half hour later, they were pulling up to the spot where Leroy told Esther to pick him up. As they slowed the car down to look for him, a figure about half a block away stepped off the curb into the street, waving his arms at them. It was Leroy. Esther's heart seemed to leap inside her chest at the sight of him, and she realized how much she loved him, more than anything else on earth.

Leroy had a slender build, not an ounce of fat on him. He excelled at playing basketball and was well-known on the basketball court in his neighborhood. It was playing basketball that kept him in shape and slowed down the destruction that heroin was doing to his body.

Grandmother saw him at the same time. Esther pointed her finger and said, "There he is." Grandmother drove the car slowly up to where Leroy was standing and came to a stop. Esther was sitting near the passenger door. She slid over next to grandmother so Leroy could have her spot in the front seat. Leroy opened the door of the Chrysler Town and Country station wagon, hopped in the car, and landed next to Esther. He said, "Hey baby," then leaned over and kissed her on the mouth. It was not the kind of kiss he wanted to greet her with, but he figured it best to wait until they were alone to express his passion for how glad he was to see her. Leroy spoke to Esther's mother, "Hi, Mrs. McAlister, thanks for picking me up."

"Don't mention it," said grandmother. "From here, I have to pick up my husband, so it's no problem at all. I'm just happy to see you're out of jail."

"God knows I'm happy to get out of that place," he said. "If the police don't kill you, the inmates will. Thanks again for getting me out. Robert Perkins told me how the two of you got your church to get him to defend me. If I'd gotten stuck with a public defender, I'd still be in jail. Not that I might not still go to jail, but Mr. Perkins was able to get me out on a thousand-dollar bail. I have a much better chance of winning my case with him defending me than I do with a public defender."

Esther interrupted him, "We need to talk about something. I've decided to quit using drugs, and I'm gonna enroll in a rehabilitation program. If we're gonna be together, I need you to quit using drugs too. Otherwise, we can't be together if you're using drugs while I'm trying to quit."

Leroy asked, "Can't we talk about this later, after we get home? I just got out of jail, and you're hitting me in the face with this crap. Can't it at least wait until after we make love before we talk about it? That reminds me, I'm out of cigarettes, Mrs. McAlister. Would you mind stopping at a store so I can get some cigarettes?"

Esther spoke up. "I've got a whole carton of cigarettes back at the hotel. You'll just have to wait till then. You know you can't be smoking in my mother's car while she's driving."

"Well, I've waited this long," said Leroy.

A short while later, the station wagon pulled up to their hotel. Esther and Leroy thanked grandmother for all that she had done, then got out and said goodbye.

Grandmother drove off to pick up grandfather from his job, where he worked as a custodian for the Los Angeles County General Hospital. She believed one of the reasons she liked the television show General Hospital so much was because her husband worked at the place during the daytime. At night, he would put mops, brooms, buckets, and all kinds of cleaning equipment into the back of their station wagon, then pick up his crew of three men who would help him clean up places.

Grandfather was trying to get his own janitorial service going, where he would charge people to clean up their buildings at night. The more contracts he could get, the more people he would hire, and if he could get enough contracts, he would just go from one job to the other, making sure the work was being done right. He dreamt of the day when he'd hardly do any of the work himself and would go from job to job, making sure others were doing a good job.

Grandmother arrived at the back entrance to General Hospital, where grandfather would soon be exiting the building. Grandmother was early, so she sat there patiently, listening to the radio while she watched employees go in and out of the door grandfather would soon be coming out of.

Every time the door opened, she'd look to see if it was grandfather coming out, hoping he'd gotten off work early. She remembered what it was like when he first started working at the hospital, and she began to reminisce. In her mind, she went over events from the last thirty years and became lost in reverie when suddenly the car door opened on the passenger side, and grandfather was getting inside the station wagon.

"Whoooo Lord, thank God this day is over," said grandfather as he settled into the passenger side of the front seat. Grandmother looked at him and asked, "You wanna drive, or you want me to drive?"

"Hell no, I don't wanna drive," said grandfather in a snarky tone of voice. "I just wanna sit back, relax, and enjoy life before I have to go to my next job. If I wanted to drive, I wouldn't have gotten in on the passenger side."

Grandmother drove off. She wanted to ask him, "How was your day?" but she knew how his day was from the statement he made when he got into the station wagon. She figured she'd try to engage in small talk, hoping it would put him in a good mood. "Leroy's out of jail," she said, wishing he would respond with "Thank God for that."

Instead, grandfather acted as if he didn't care and asked, "What's for dinner when we get home?"

"I got a pot roast in the oven, with potatoes, carrots, and a side dish of macaroni and cheese with cornbread and collard greens, waiting for us when we get home," said grandmother.

Grandfather would eat dinner and watch The Evening News on TV when he got home. After the news, he'd relax in his big, easy chair for a while and watch Star Trek reruns before he would get the mops, buckets, and cleaning equipment loaded into the back of the station wagon. He was always able to get whatever supplies he needed at a discount, if not free, from where he worked at General Hospital because he was the supervisor of maintenance on the day shift at the hospital.

About nine, nine-thirty, he'd head out to pick up his cleaning crew, which consisted of Arthur, Bob, and Ron. Arthur was one of grandfather's best friends. They'd known each other for years. Arthur used to work at General Hospital with grandfather years ago but was fired for showing up at work under the influence of alcohol.

It was no secret he had a drinking problem, one that had seen him in and out of AA for many years. He would get sober for a while but always seemed to go back to drinking. Arthur was a fifty-five-year-old bachelor who had no children and was not gay. He was about six feet tall, two hundred pounds, had a thick mustache, and a huge bald spot. His friends said he looked like the actor Moses Gunn. Grandmother believed if the right woman tried to help him quit drinking, he would be able to quit. She thought that all the times he went to AA, he was secretly hoping to find a mate, someone who could help him stay sober. But a friend had told her AA doesn't work that way—you have to get sober by yourself.

AA can support, encourage, and give you a road map to sobriety, but you have to do the work yourself. Grandmother tried to get him to come to her church, hoping he could meet someone there. "The church is a great place for a fifty-five-year-old bachelor to find a wife," grandmother would say to grandfather. Grandfather would try not to laugh whenever she said it, and at one point, he replied, "That's probably why he never goes to church."

On one occasion, grandmother asked Arthur why he had never married. He replied by saying, "Not one of the women I wanted to marry were women who wanted to marry me, and the only women that wanted to marry me were women I did not want to marry."

Bob was an unemployed black man who dropped out of high school and was a friend of the family. He was about average height and weight, not good looking, nor was he what you'd call ugly. He had known grandfather since he was in grade school, and now that he was a young adult in his early twenties he had a hard time finding a job with less than a high school education.

Bob was someone who hated going to school. When he was in school the other kids used to call him stupid. On many occasions when a room full of students would gather together someone would ask, "Who's the dumbest one here?" Suddenly, the room would become quiet, and although no one would say anything, everyone would look at Bob, and it was clear that everyone considered him the dumbest person there. Bob had a learning disability and had no idea he was dyslexic. He had trouble reading, and writing, and his math was worse than his reading or writing because his being dyslexic would cause him to write numbers in a different order than he saw them on the page. Thus if the equation was 24 + 32 he would write down 42+ 32 or 24+23, not knowing his dyslexia was causing him to see the numbers in reverse order.

To make matters worse he could not speak english without mispronouncing words which made him seem more illiterate than he was. He had a habit of pronouncing words that began with the letter 'T' with a 'D.' Instead of saying this or that, he would say dhis or dhat. Certain words that began with the letter 'S,' he would pronounce with a 'th' sound. Instead of saying the word 'suppose,' he would pronounce it as thapose.

One of his teachers claimed he suffered from what was called a lazy tongue; whenever he said a word like "this or that," his tongue was supposed to touch his teeth in order to produce the 'th," sound, but his tongue never touched his teeth, Instead, it touched his gums right behind his teeth, which caused him to speak with a disfluency or a speech disorder. The teacher said he needed to see a speech therapist, but the school did not have a speech therapist, and no one could afford to pay for a speech therapist to teach Bob how to pronounce words the right way, so he never learned to articulate the English language the way a normal person does.

Ron was a white man in his mid mid-thirties. He had recently fallen on hard times and needed any kind of work he could find to make money until he could get a real job as a musician. Ron was one of those white musicians who loved to play jazz, his parents were poor and he'd grown up among black people from the time he was in elementary school. He was good at playing basketball, which made him popular among black people who liked to play basketball.

Playing basketball kept him in great shape, and he always was in good shape. When he was growing up he used to love what was called the Motown Sound, but as he got older, the blues, jazz and rock and roll became his favorite kinds of music. He used to say the blues was the father of jazz, soul and rock and roll, but you can't make any money as a musician if you're playing the blues.

He claimed rock and roll musicians made the most money, but you had to get established in the field of recognition before you could make any money at it and there were more musicians playing rock and roll music than there were musicians playing any other kind of music. For Ron, jazz was the kind of music he enjoyed playing more than rock and roll, even more than the blues. The way Ron played jazz was like an advanced form of the blues ; you could still hear elements of the blues in the music he played, but it was the offspring of it you were listening to. It was jazz, not the blues.

About nine o:'clock, grandfather would have loaded his cleaning equipment, namely mops, buckets, brooms, wax and soap, into the station wagon. Then he'd pick up his cleaning crew, from there they would go to different locations on different nights to clean up. Grandfather specialized in cleaning floors, he had an electric buffer for making floors shine after he waxed them. He had a rug shampooer for cleaning carpets, and most of his clients would only need him once a month to shampoo their carpets.

Tower records Records was one of his biggest clients. He would go to different Tower Records stores on different nights and strip the old wax off the floor and put down new wax. Other places he had were office buildings. The offices would need to be vacuumed and the trash emptied five nights a week, and the carpets he would need to shampoo once a month. There were about two or three restaurants whose floors he would strip and wax, but they were not as big as Tower Records.

Arthur, or Art, as everyone called him, had been working with grandfather longer than anyone else. He knew what places they were going to clean up on what nights of the week. The office buildings came first. It didn't take long to vacuum and empty the trash then came Tower Records. Bob and Ron enjoyed working at Tower Records. They loved to look at the posters and album covers while they worked. It allowed them to keep abreast of the new releases in their favorite field of music. The store manager was there while they stripped and waxed the floor and would play the latest records for them while they worked.

As they were on their way to Tower Records, the station wagon came to a stop at a red light. There were prostitutes standing on the corner and one of the prostitutes started waving at them. She looked to be in her early twenties, a light -skinned black woman slightly darker than the shade of a paper bag. The woman was extremely attractive, dressed in a patent leather mini -skirt with a matching waist-length jacket, a netted see-through blouse and fishnet stockings. As they drove by, she shouted, "Hey baby, you want some of this," she then raised up her skirt high enough for them to see she wasn't wearing any panties.

Arthur was sitting in the front passenger seat. He looked at her and said, "She doesn't look that bad."

Bob was sitting in the seat behind the driver's seat. He leaned forward, then backward, trying to look around Ron, who was sitting behind Arthur. "Damm, Ron, move your head back tho I can thee,."

"If you wanna see her that bad, get out the car and go talk to her," said Ron.

The light turned green, and grandfather drove off, happy to get away from what was known as, "Whores Corner"

"Hey Art, you think you might go back and get that after work," Ron said in a joking manner.

"Don't ask me," said Arthur, "Ask Bob, he's the one who wanted to get out of the car and talk to her."

"Uuh uh," said Bob.

"Don't put dhat lie on me, I just wanted to get a good look at her and thee what thee looked like."

"What's it called when three or more prostitutes are standing on the same corner,?" asked Ron,.

"I don't know. What's it called?" replied Arthur?.

"A whoe sale," said Ron.

"That makes sense," said Arthur," "They're sure to lower their price in order to compete with each other."

"Art, you sure theem tha know a lot about how prostitutes charge people, theems like you're talking from experience," said Bob.

"It doesn't take experience, all it takes is understanding the laws of supply and demand," replied Arthur.

"Yeh, and dhey thupply your demands at a price you can afford, is dhat it," said Bob in a retorted.

"Man, I'm not gonna lie to you," said Arthur, "I'm fifty fifty-five years old, and there have been times when I've paid a woman to have sex with me, but it was not any of those pavement princesses we just passed standing on the corner. There was a time when I thought I'd never pay for a woman to have sex with me, but reality changes as you get older, and the older you get, the more reality changes."

"How old are you?," Art asked.

"I'm dhwenty-four years old," answered Bob, "And I ain't never bought no pussy in my life and never will."

Arthur took a deep breath. He glanced over at grandfather, who was driving and seemed to be pretending his driving was what kept him exempt from the conversation going on.

He then looked back over his shoulder at Bob in the back seat and said, "Prostitution is the oldest profession known to man, prostitution is illegal in the state of California, and yet we just drove by a place where prostitutes were standing on the corner trying to sell us some pussy. As long as a man is willing to pay a woman to let him fuck her and a woman is willing to accept money for letting him stick his dick in her, there is no way you or I or the government of the United States, or the Lord God Almighty for that matter, will bring an end to prostitution in our society, and it all boils down to the basic laws of supply and demand, or as you put it, a prostitute will supply your demands at a price you can afford. So take yo baptist ass back to church where it's a sin to pay for sex, and get married to some big ass sloppy bitch that the church wants you to take care of because you'll go to hell if you pay a woman to let you stick your dick in her."

Ron bursted out in laughter, after he finished laughing, he said, ""I love it, I love it, I just love it. Art has had sex with prostitutes but doesn't want to admit it. Bob has never paid a woman to have sex with him, Geary has been happily married for god knows how long, and I'm a musician. How in the hell did I end up here? "

Ron went back to laughing as if he were the only person aware of what reality truly is. Gradually, his laughter came to an ending, and he began to speak, but it was clear he was talking to himself more than anyone else. He said,"I have been to Spain, I have been to Tokyo, I have been to Africa and Ohio, I never try to get in the news. I'm just a man who is crying the blues." He then paused briefly and asked, "Does anybody in this car know that song?"

Well, that's how I feel right now because, as a musician, I got a chance to go to Amsterdam. Prostitution in Europe is nothing like it is here in the United States, and in Amsterdam, prostitution is not like anything I've seen anywhere in the world. You can go window shopping for a prostitute in Amsterdam the same way people go window shopping at Sears or Macy's.

"Tho you're thaying prostitution is okay and ain't nothing wrong with being a prostitute," said Bob.

"I'm saying Art is right about supply and demand, and as long as there's a demand for it, the government is not gonna stop it by making it illegal," said Ron.

"By making it legal, the government will be able to control it. In Europe, the prostitutes have to go to a clinic once a month and get a check-up to make sure they're not carrying any disease. The whores in Europe are a lot cleaner than the ones standing on the corner we just passed. Another thing is if the police were to arrest the prostitutes we just saw and stop them from standing on the corner, prostitution would just show up somewhere else. By making it legal, the government is able to contain prostitution to a certain area."

"Well, if dhat's dha case, you might as well legalize drugs," said Bob. "Because dha thame thing with thapply and daman applies tha drugs."

Arthur jumped in and said, "You've got a much better chance of stopping drugs than you do of stopping prostitution, but I see your point, and it's a good one."

"As long as there's a demand for drugs, people are gonna get high, but the thing about drugs is if you can cut off the supply, you can stop people from using 'em."

Ron spoke up and said, "Remember what happened during Prohibition? The government made alcohol illegal, and people kept on drinking it, bathtub gin, and wood alcohol. People were dying left and right from drinking homemade alcohol until Roosevelt made it legal. After he made it legal, they could regulate it. People stopped dying from homemade alcohol."

"Yeah," said Arthur, "And the reason Roosevelt made it legal was so he could put a tax on it. He was trying to get the country out of the depression. I was born in 1916, when they legalized alcohol, I was 17 years old . I remember Roosevelt, I remember the depression." Arthur looked at grandfather and said "Geary, you're older than me. How old were you when they ended prohibition?"

Grandfather said, "I was 28 years old in 1933, and I remember Roosevelt too, but they weren't born then, so they don't know nothing about it. They have no idea what it was like, how bad things were before Roosevelt took over."

Ron spoke up and said, "I'm thirty-two years old, and Bob is the youngest one in the car; he's twenty four."

Bob said, "I'm old enough to vote, drink, and go tha Vietnam."

"You were born in 1948," said Ron. "I was born in 1938, so I ain't worried about going to Vietnam."

"I tell yeah," said Arthur, "Y'all stand a much better chance of coming back alive from Vietnam than we did of coming back from World War II. There was a place called Omaha Beach in Normandy. When we landed on that beach, everyone knew the first wave was gonna get killed. I mean, we were getting wiped out before we even made it to the beach, and if you did make it out of the water and were lucky enough to get to dry land, it was pure hell. The Germans knew we were coming and had set up barbed wire all along the beach, making it almost impossible to go forward. And when you tried to dig into the sand, they had dumped broken concrete all over the beach and covered it up with sand. So you couldn't dig in and you couldn't go forward, and you couldn't go back; behind you were thousands of soldiers trying to make it to dry land, and they were worse off than you. The water in the ocean was so full of blood that the waves that came up onto the shore were red, red from the blood of American soldiers. The ocean was full of dead bodies."

American soldiers had to make their way through them to get to land, and when you got to land, your best bet was to grab a dead body and use it for cover to stay alive. The beach led up to a high cliff, and on top of the cliff, the Germans had cannons, and my god, did they have a lot of cannons. The air support was supposed to have taken out the cannons before we landed on the beach, but because of the bad weather, they didn't. They finally did show up, and we finally made it through the barbed wire and metal spikes, but if you were the last man to hit the beach, you were lucky to be alive; if you were one of the first ones to hit the beach, you got killed."

Grandfather spoke up and said, "Getting back to Roosevelt, it was World War II that got us out of the Depression. World War II put everyone to work. They had to build ships and planes, cannons, jeeps, machine guns, and ammunition. Everything that was needed to fight the Germans in World War II was built by civilians, and when the war was over, the majority of the people were better off than they were before the war. Of course, Roosevelt died before the war ended. It hurt like hell to see the president of the United States die right before the war ended. He was the one who led the country through it and did not live to see the outcome. "We have nothing to fear but fear itself."

Ron spoke up, saying, "Getting back to the subject of prostitution and drugs, in Amsterdam, they have coffee houses where you can buy and smoke marijuana. Here in the United States, marijuana is illegal and considered a drug. Compared to cocaine, meth, and heroin, marijuana is not a drug. You can smoke weed all day long, not get addicted, and never OD from smoking marijuana. As far as I'm concerned, marijuana is not a drug; marijuana is a plant, one that grows in my backyard. But when it comes to those drugs like heroin, cocaine, LSD, meth, or mescaline, that's a different story.

And I still think the government will be able to control drugs and the people who use drugs if they were to legalize them. Because if drugs were legal, the black market for drugs would disappear because the best drugs would be legally bought and sold, and the price of drugs would go down. The main reason drugs cost a lot of money is that they're illegal. If drugs were legal, people would go to clinics to shoot up, fewer people would OD, and some people would use hard drugs at home, but the government would be able to regulate the amount of drugs and regulate the people who used them."

"Yeah," said Bob, "But getting' back tah prostitution, what's dah difference between us and the prostitutes back dhere tandin' on dha corner?"

"Okay," said Arthur, "What's the difference?"

"Prostitutes get paid when dhey get fucked; we get fucked when we get paid."

For a moment, the car was quiet, then Ron spoke up and said, "You got no argument from me there. Right now, I cannot find work as a musician, and I have to do something, anything at all, to make any money I can, but as soon as I can get a gig playing keyboard, I'm sure you fellows will miss me as much as I will miss being a janitor."

"Well," said Grandfather, "there are worse things than being a janitor."

"Okay," said Ron, "name a few. How many jobs can you name that's worse than being a janitor, or should I say a custodian?"

"Go down a few blocks off Pico and Crenshaw to the corner of Pico and Norton around one a.m. until two thirty or three a.m. on a Friday or Saturday night," retorted Grandfather. "There's a place called the Catch One club where the gays and transvestites are the main patrons. The place closes right before two a.m., and at two a.m., it's the number one corner in Los Angeles for male prostitutes, and ninety percent of them are transvestites who look like women. The people looking for a male prostitute, or more specifically, a male transvestite, know what time the club lets out, and you could be standing on the corner of Norton and Pico instead of stripping and waxing floors. That's worse than being a janitor," said Grandfather.

"Being a prostitute is worse than being a janitor?" asked Ron. "Do you seriously think we make more money than prostitutes? I mean, granted, they have nights when business is bad, and they don't make much, but on a good night, a prostitute will make more money in one night than we'll make in a week, more like two weeks. As a janitor, we're at the very bottom of the pay scale. When you talk about minimum wage, you're talking about the starting pay scale of a janitor. That joke Bob told was the truth: 'Prostitutes get paid when they get fucked; minimum wage workers get fucked when they get paid.'"

"Well," replied Grandfather, "if you can make more money as a prostitute, why aren't you out there standing on the corner of Norton and Pico at one and two o'clock in the morning where you can get paid for sucking dick and gettin' fucked in the ass instead of working as a janitor?"

"First and foremost," exclaimed Ron, ""I am not a transvestite . I like women, I am not into sucking dick or getting fucked in the ass, and if I could get paid for having sex with women, I'd do it, but the only women I'd have sex with would be the women who appealed to me. If I were a prostitute, I'd have to fuck some three hundred pound bitch who was so ugly the only way she could get laid was to pay somebody to fuck her. I'd rather be a janitor than have to stick my dick in something like that, and there ain't enough money to make me go down on some big fat sloppy bitch who I refuse to stick my dick in."

"So being a janitor is better than being a prostitute,'" grandfather asked?

"Well," said Ron, "I can't speak for other people. All I can say is, 'to each his own.' If you were to ask any one of those prostitutes standing on the corner back there if being a janitor is worse than being a prostitute, they'd say yeah, and so would the transvestites standing outside the Catch One at two o'clock in the morning. You know damn well a prostitute would rather suck dick and get fucked in the ass than mop floors and clean toilets."

Bob spoke up, saying, "You know they're all going tah hell. Each and every one of 'em is going tah hell."

"Oh no," chimed Arthur, "please don't start with that religious bullshit."

"Well, it's true," said Bob. "You may not wanah admit it, but their souls belong to dah devil. You see those prostitutes back there? They all got a demon in 'em. They are Satan's daughters, and they're going tah hell, just like all those people who went to Woodstock when they had that big rock concert in New York a few years ago. There were people running around naked saying 'Free Love,' and all of 'em, or just about all of 'em, were taking drugs.

Most of 'em were taking LSD. It was all over the news. I seen it on T.V. And my Pastor talked about it in church. There were five hundred thousand young people at that concert, and all of 'em are going tah hell."

"And did he tell you that rock and roll music was the devil's music?" asked Ron.

"Well," said Bob, "thome of it, not all of it, but thome of it is dah devil's music, like dah Beatles song, 'He'll hold you in his arms till you can feel his disease.' Now daht's dah devil's music."

"Oh no," Arthur yelled out, while at the same time, Ron started singing, "Come together, right now, over me."

Ron came to an abrupt stop, as if something suddenly occurred to him. He turned to Bob and said, "A minute ago, you said that all of the young people who went to Woodstock had a demon in them and they were going tah hell."

Bob interrupted him, saying, "I said that dah prostitutes standing on dah corner had demons in 'em, but now that you bring it up, the young people who didn't have a demon in 'em when they came to the concert, day all had a demon in 'em when they left."

Ron spoke up and said, "Forget about the prostitutes. You're saying that people who did not have a demon in 'em when they came to the concert had a demon in 'em when they left."

Bob agreed and said, "Dats right."

Ron asked, "Did the people who went to the concert without a demon in them know they had a demon in them after they left the concert, or did they know they were getting a demon put in them while they were at the concert?"

Bob hunched his shoulders and said, "All I know is dhey all had demons in 'em."

Ron asked Bob, "Is it possible for a person to have a demon inside of them and not know that there is a demon inside of them?"

Bob said, "Yeah, I guess so."

Ron asked, "Is it possible for you to have a demon in you and not know it?"

Bob replied, "No, it ain't possible for me tah have a demon in me and not know it. If anything, I have an angel inside me because I'm a child of God doing the Lord's work on earth."

"Well, you might not know it," said Ron, "but you and everyone on this planet has a demon inside them. Everyone has an uncontrollable voice inside their head that speaks to them at any given moment; it's called a demon. There are two kinds of people: those who know they have a demon in them and those who don't, and you're one of those who don't know they have a demon in them. Religion is a means of putting a bridle on the demon inside us."

At this point, Bob could not conceal his anger and couldn't help raising his voice as he lashed out, "You mean tah tell me dhat dha pastor of my church, Reverend Johnson, has a demon in him? You gonna sit dhere and tell me dhat Dr. Martin Luther King Jr. had a demon in him? I know dhat everybody has a guardian angel, and your guardian angel is not gonna let a demon get inside you unless you betray your guardian angel and want a demon tah get inside you. Anybody who believes in Jesus will not have a demon inside 'em because Jesus will not allow a demon to get inside of anybody who believes in him."

Ron replied, "That's what the demon inside you wants you to think."

Bob didn't answer. He sat there with his head down and his eyes closed, trying to keep his composure. After about thirty seconds, Bob started speaking so fast it was hard to comprehend what he was saying. "You dha devil," said Bob, "you ain't nothing but the devil because dhat's what dha devil wants: for everybody to have a demon in 'em."

Grandfather drove the car into the parking lot of the Tower Records building they were going to clean up. He came to a stop near the entrance. Everyone got out of the station wagon and started unloading brooms, mops, and buckets from the back. The store was closed, but the manager and the employees were still there. The store employees were leaving at the same time grandfather arrived; only the store manager remained until the floors had been cleaned, and it was time to lock up the building.

The manager unlocked the door to let grandfather and his cleaning crew inside. Once inside, they started sweeping the floors. After the floors were swept, they'd empty the waste baskets into a huge trash bin outside in the back of the store. After the trash was emptied, they'd mop the floor, wait for it to dry, then put down a coat of wax. Afterward, they'd wait for the first coat of wax to dry before applying a second coat.

While they were waiting for the floor to dry, Bob and Ron would go outside to smoke a cigarette. Grandfather and Arthur would place huge fans in certain locations and turn them on. The wind circulating from the fans would cause the floor to dry much quicker. After they turned the fans on, they'd go outside and join Bob and Ron.

Bob asked grandfather why he never went to church on Sunday. Bob was a member of Reverend Johnson's church, the same church grandmother went to. One Sunday, Bob's mother was talking to grandmother and mentioned how her son was having a hard time finding a job. The next thing you know, grandmother had talked grandfather into giving Bob a job as part of his cleaning crew. Grandfather did not regret giving Bob a job. He was a good worker, but there were things about Bob that caused grandfather to feel uneasy. Grandfather got used to the way Bob mispronounced words, but there were times when Arthur and Ron made fun of Bob for having less than average intelligence, and then there were Bob's religious beliefs.

Bob was one of those persons who just assumed that everyone he came in contact with realized there was a God who created the universe and everything in it. Grandfather did not believe in God the same way Bob believed in God. So when Bob asked grandfather why he never went to church on Sunday, grandfather felt Bob would not understand how he saw God compared to the way Bob saw God, but he felt he had to give Bob an answer.

"Well," said grandfather, "to answer your question, you don't have to go to church to worship God. God and the church are two different things, and then there's Jesus. God and Jesus are two different things, although there are people who believe God walked the earth inside of Jesus and…"

Before grandfather could finish what he was saying, Bob interrupted him, never aware that he cut him off and said, "Yeah, dhat's who Jesus was. Jesus was God in dha form of a human being, cause in dha book of John it thays, 'In dha beginning was dha Word, and dha Word was God,' and it goes on ta thay, 'He was in dha world, and dha world was made by Him, and dha world knew Him not.' Later on it thays, 'Dha Word was made flesh and dwelt among us,' and last but not least, it thays dhat Jesus Himself ted, 'I and dha Father are one.' Dhat's why I thay dhere are other places in dha Bible where it talks about Jesus as God, but dha book of John is clear dhat God was on earth, and He was on earth as Jesus."

Grandfather said, "I'm not gonna argue with you. Every person has a right to believe whatever they wanna believe. Like I was saying, there are people who believe God walked the earth as Jesus, and there are Christians who believe Jesus was not God but a man."

Once again, Bob interrupted grandfather while he was talking. Bob was one of those kinds of people who would interrupt whenever a person said something he wanted to respond to. It never occurred to him to wait until the person who was talking finished what they were saying before he said what he had to say. He had no idea he was being rude when he suddenly started talking before the person who was speaking finished. Little did he know how annoying he was by constantly interrupting grandfather in the middle of his sentence.

"Yeah," exclaimed Bob, "a lot of Christians see Jesus as dha Son of God, but dhey don't know Jesus was God. I mean, it's okay ta worship Jesus as dha Son of God because dhat's dha only way you can get into heaven. If you don't accept Jesus as your savior, you're not gonna go to heaven when you die, and even if you do accept Jesus as your savior, you have to live your life without sin in order to get into heaven, cause it says in dha Bible, 'Faith without works is dead.' And a lot of people just don't realize dhat when dhey are worshiping Jesus, dhey are worshiping God through Jesus because Jesus is God."

Grandfather decided to give up trying to answer the question Bob had asked him because every time he tried to answer it, Bob would interrupt him and continue to talk as if he couldn't care less about why grandfather didn't go to church on Sunday. Grandfather saw Bob as one of those people who loved to talk but could care less about listening to what other people had to say. He had started the conversation by asking grandfather a question and would interrupt grandfather every time he tried to answer it.

It was as if, during the middle of a sentence, Bob would decide to interrupt and say something short. Only instead of saying something short that could be said in one sentence, it would turn into a paragraph, and the paragraph would turn into a page of words before he finished talking. Grandfather felt it was best not to go back to the beginning of the conversation; that would be like turning pages backward in a book, so he just picked up the conversation where Bob left off.

"So, in other words, when God is on earth, God is Jesus, but when God is not on earth, God is Yahweh or Jehovah or Allah, is that what you're saying?"

"Yeah," said Bob, "I never looked at it like dhat, but I guess you could thay dhat."

"And in order to go to heaven, you have to accept Jesus as your savior or else you won't go tah heaven."

"Yeah, dhat's right," said Bob. "Dha only way unto dha Father is true Jesus."

"So if a person worships Yahweh or Jehovah or Allah and does all the things God tells them to do but does not accept Jesus as their savior, will that person get to go to heaven when they die?"

"No, dhat person will not get into heaven when dhey die unless dhey accept Jesus as dheir Lord and Savior."

"So all the Muslims, all the Jews, all the Hindus, all the Buddhists, ain't none of them going to heaven because they don't accept Jesus as their savior?"

Bob said, "Dhose are all false religions. Dha only true religion is tah worship God through Jesus because God is so great. Dhat's the only way we can come in tha God's grace, true Jesus. Without Jesus, we would be destroyed by dha power and dha glory of God if we were to come anywhere near Him. But when God came to earth as Jesus, it allowed us tah worship God directly true Jesus. When Jesus got crucified, God was inside of Jesus when He was crucified, and dha blood of Jesus is also dha blood of God when He walked dha earth as a human being. When we accept Jesus as our savior, we become washed clean of our sins, true dha blood dhat was shed at his crucifixion, and dhat's dha only way we can get into heaven. Dhat's why all other religions are false religions."

"Okay, let me put it another way," said Grandfather. "If a person is good and does not do anything wrong, but does not believe Jesus is the Son of God and does not accept Jesus as their savior, will that person go to hell simply because they don't accept Jesus as their savior?"

"I don't know if dhey'll go tah hell, but dhey won't go tah heaven," said Bob.

"So you're saying heaven is reserved for Christians only, and no matter how much good a person does, they won't get into heaven unless they believe in Jesus and accept him as their savior," replied Grandfather.

"Yeah," said Bob, "dhat's about what it comes down to, cause all other religions are false, and dha only way you can get tah God is true Jesus."

"Okay," said Grandfather. "You mentioned that concert they held a few years ago and said everyone who went to that concert was going to hell. About a month before that concert, they had a riot in New York at a place called 'Stonewall.' My wife and I watch the news every evening; otherwise, I'd have never known anything about it. Have you ever heard of the 'Stonewall Riots' in New York City?"

"No," said Bob. "I live in Los Angeles. I don't live in New York. I can tell you about dha Watts riots we had here in Los Angeles a few years ago."

"The Stonewall riot happened in New York when the police raided a homosexual nightclub, and the homosexuals in the nightclub started a riot. Since then, the homosexuals have started to get organized and are asking for something they call 'Gay Rights.' So what does the Bible say about people who are homosexuals?" asked Grandfather. "According to the Bible, are people who are homosexuals going to be able to get into heaven?"

"Dhey going tah hell," said Bob. "All homosexuals are agents of dha devil. Some of um might not know it, but all homosexuals are a part of dha devil's plan to destroy mankind. Each homosexual has to go out and turn someone who is not a homosexual into one, and when all dha men have sex with men and all dha women have sex with women, won't no children be born, and it'll be dha end of all mankind. Homosexuals love to have sex with someone who is not a homosexual because dhey know dhey are turning someone into a homosexual like dim. Homosexuality is an abomination to dha Lord."

"Okay," said Grandfather, "but what exactly does the Bible say about homosexuals?"

"It says dey're an abomination to dha Lord!" exclaimed Bob.

Grandfather looked at Bob with an intense look upon his face and asked, "Do you know who James Baldwin is?"

"James Baldwin is a writer. He's a black man who's a writer. I haven't read any of his books, but I know who he is," said Bob.

"You're right. He's a writer, but James Baldwin is more than just a writer. He was a close friend of Dr. Martin Luther King Jr., and he's very much involved in the civil rights movement. He never hurt anyone or did anything wrong, and he's a homosexual. Are you telling me James Baldwin is going to hell because he's a homosexual?"

Bob started to speak, but Grandfather wasn't finished and cut him off. "Are you telling me that God saw James Baldwin as an abomination because he was a homosexual when Dr. Martin Luther King Jr. saw him as a close friend?"

Bob started to speak and said, "Dha Bible says…"

Grandfather interrupted and said, "The Bible was written by men, not God—men who claimed that what they wrote was the word of God because it was inspired by God. We have nothing that was written by God, but you and a lot of other people believe the Bible is the word of God when God didn't write one page, one sentence, one word that is in the Bible. Now here's what pisses me off: you say that God walked the earth inside of Jesus and…"

Bob tried to speak, but Grandfather told him, "Shut up." Then Grandfather continued talking.

"And if God were inside of Jesus, why didn't Jesus write the New Testament? If Jesus had written the New Testament, you could say it was written by God because God was in Jesus when he wrote it, but we don't have one thing that was written by Jesus. All of the New Testament is based on hearsay; not one page of the New Testament was written by anyone who was with Jesus while he was alive. The book of Mark was not written by the disciple Mark; the book of Matthew was not written by the disciple Matthew, and the book of John was not written by the disciple John. And you ask me why I don't go to church on Sunday."

"Forget about James Baldwin," said Bob. "What about Sammy Davis Jr.? He quit being a Christian and became a Jew. Both him and James Baldwin are going tah hell."

"That's it," said Grandfather. "The floor's dry, and we can get the hell out of here."

Grandfather realized Bob was not going to see reality in the context of "ipso facto." If it is a fact, it is so. To Grandfather, the truth was determined by whatever the facts were. The words "existential reality" were the highest criteria for determining what the truth was, and he felt there was no use talking to him. Bob was a good worker, but he lived in a reality based on a belief, not based on the facts. Anything that did not support his beliefs, he could not accept.

But when Bob started talking about Sammy Davis Jr. going to hell, it really upset and angered Grandfather. Sammy Davis Jr. was one of Grandfather's favorite actors. Grandfather loved Sammy Davis Jr, and for Bob to say that Sammy Davis Jr. was going to hell because he became a Jew and was no longer a Christian was something Grandfather could not fathom.

Bob spoke up, saying, "I know your wife, Mrs. McAllister, is a Christian. I'm pretty sure she's going tah heaven. Up until now, I thought you was a Christian, but I know dhat everyone who's a Christian ain't going tah heaven, and I don't think you gonna make it."

Grandfather began gathering up the mops and the mop buckets. Bob automatically grabbed brooms and dustpans. They took them outside, where Arthur and Ron were. They had finished smoking and were just talking. When they saw Grandfather and Bob bringing the cleaning equipment out of the store, they knew it was time to go. They quickly piled all the cleaning equipment into the station wagon, got inside, and drove off.

By now, the anger Grandfather felt when Bob said Sammy Davis Jr. was going to hell had subsided. Grandfather wanted to finish the conversation he was having with Bob, and he told him, "Just because a person's religious beliefs are different than yours does not mean that person is going to hell."

He told Bob he had come up with his own religious beliefs, one in which he was still a Christian because he instilled a lot of the Christian teachings into his beliefs. At the same time, there were many things he did not accept in Christianity, such as Jesus being the Son of God, or the Virgin Mary really being a virgin, Jesus walking on water, or raising the dead. Grandfather told Bob that if he asked a hundred different people to give him their definition of God, he would end up with a hundred different definitions of what

God is. According to the church, their definition of God is the only true definition of God; everyone else is wrong.

"I refuse to allow the church to tell me that how I see God is wrong and that they have a monopoly on the existence of God and how a person should see God. So, I have my own religion. In my religion, there is a spark of the divine being in each and every one of us. A small part of God exists inside of you and me; some people call it a spirit, some call it a soul. Some say the soul and the spirit are the same thing; others say the soul and the spirit are two different things. But whether you call it a soul or a spirit, it connects us to God. And in my religion, there are times when God is able to move that spirit, that soul inside us in a way that only He can move it."

"I agree with you about dha spirit of God being inside of all of us, but dha Holy Bible is dha book dhat tells us how God wants us to worship him, and dha church is dha house of God because dha church tells us how dha Bible wants us to worship God," said Bob.

"Do you believe everything in the Bible is true?" asked Grandfather.

"Yeah, I believe it," said Bob. "Dha Bible is a book dhat's holy, so everything in it got to be true."

"Well," said Grandfather, "in the book of Judges, there is a place in the Bible where the sun stands still over the earth because the Hebrew people, led by Moses, needed more daylight. So God stopped the sun from going down until they had finished fighting a battle. And in the book of Isaiah, not only does the earth stop turning, but the sun goes backward ten degrees."

In order for that to happen, the earth would have to come to a complete stop, then go backward ten degrees, come to a complete stop a second time, and then start to rotate forward. That's impossible, but it's in the Bible because the people who wrote the Bible believed the earth was flat and that the sun, the moon, and the stars went around the earth. To them, the earth was the center of everything, and they had no idea how big the universe really is. To them, the universe consisted of the earth, the sun, the stars, and the moon. They had no idea how big the universe or even the solar system was. They thought the planet Venus was a wandering star. If you were to tell the people who wrote the Bible that the earth was round and that it went around the sun, they would have called you a heretic and probably would have burned you at the stake."

Ron spoke up and said, "Galileo was lucky they didn't kill him for saying the earth went around the sun."

Arthur commented on Galileo by saying, "Galileo was a well-known, respected scientist who invented the telescope. If it had been you or I who said it, they would have killed us. However, they did put a sword to Galileo's throat and made him say the sun went around the earth. But I still say they would have killed us if any of us had said it back in those days."

Bob spoke up, saying, "Everybody taught dha world was flat until Columbus came along?"

"You're missing the point," said Grandfather. "The point is the earth did not stand still like it says in the Bible."

"The Bible is still the book that tells us how God wants us to worship Him," said Bob.

"The Bible is a book written by men to convince other men to worship god the way they wanted us to."said grandfather.

"You believe in the Bible," asked Grandfather?

"There's a place in the book of Genesis where Jacob had two sons, Simeon and Levi. Now, in the story, Jacob comes to a city in the land of Canaan and sets up camp outside the city. Jacob's daughter Dinah goes into the city and ends up having sex with the son of the person who is the ruler of the city. The son of the ruler wants to marry Jacob's daughter, Dinah, and Jacob's sons tell him that, in order to marry their sister, he and every other male in his city must become circumcised.

The prince of the city agrees. He and all the men in the city become circumcised. On the third day, after all the men have been circumcised and soreness has set in, two of the sons of Jacob, Simeon and Levi, go into the city and kill every man in the entire city. There are a lot of other things in this story that are not right, but for just two men to kill every man in an entire city does not sound possible. It would take more than two men to kill an entire city of men, and none of the men could fight back because their foreskins had been cut off.

Afterward, they loot the city and take everything of value, including the wives and children of the men they killed. The men Simeon and Levi killed were innocent people who had nothing to do with the prince of the city having sex with their sister, Dinah. The Bible does not say if the sex was consensual, so we don't know if it was a case of rape. We only know the sons of Jacob lied about the men being circumcised in order to marry their sister so they could kill all of them and sack the city."

"After Moses died, Joshua led the people to the Promised Land. When they reached the Promised Land, there were people living on it. God told Joshua to kill the people living in the Promised Land. I can go on about things in the Bible where God did something that was not right, but I won't talk about them or about what God did to Job."

"Then there's King David," said Grandfather.

"What about King David?" asked Bob.

"According to you, King David is going to hell because he had a homosexual relationship with Jonathan, the son of King Saul."

"King David was not a homosexual," retorted Bob. "He had more dhan one wife and a bunch of children."

"Yeah," said Grandfather, "and he also had a homosexual affair with a man named Jonathan. It says in the Bible that David loved Jonathan more than he loved any woman."

Arthur chimed in, saying, "Wait a minute, I know all about that. David was not a homosexual, but Jonathan, the son of King Saul, was. Jonathan had fallen in love with David and at that time David was a hero for killing Goliath. Jonathan was a prince the son of a king, and he ordered David to lay down on these giant pillows and not move while he did something to him. So David laid down on the pillows and after he laid down Jonathan took off all his cloths and gave him a blow job and after the blow job David took off all his cloths and David ended up becoming bisexual from having sex with Jonathan.

There's this part in the Bible where King Saul gets mad at David and throws a spear at him. After that, he ends up chasing David all over the Middle East.

Here's what really happened: David and Jonathan were in the middle of committing a sexual act on each other, and King Saul walked in on them. When Saul saw what they were doing, he wanted to become part of their act, or rather, he wanted David to become part of his act, but David was not gonna perform the act with King Saul. David made it clear that Jonathan was the only male he did the act with. But King Saul had a demon in him that was put there by the Lord back in the book of First Samuel."

Grandfather interrupted, saying, "If you ask me, it was wrong for the Lord to put a demon in anyone, let alone the king of anyone's people."

Arthur continued, "So the demon in Saul went crazy when he saw David and Jonathan performing their act on one another, and he lusted after David. I mean, he just had to have him.

David and Jonathan would be lying on these huge giant-size pillows, completely naked, performing their act on one another, while King Saul would be spying on them from behind some curtains, and he would masturbate the whole time he was looking at um. King Saul told David he was gonna kill him if he didn't let him have his way with him, and when David refused, that was when King Saul threw a spear at him."

"Wait a minute," said grandfather, "Where does it say in the Bible that King Saul masturbated while he was spying on David and Jonathan?" asked Grandfather.

"It ain't in the Bible," said Arthur. "But that's what I believe happened."

"If it ain't in dha Bible, dhat's because it didn't happen," said Bob.

"You don't know what you're talking about," said Arthur. "In the Bible, when David first saw Bathsheba, the mother of King Solomon, the woman's naked. The Bible doesn't tell you she was naked; it says King David looked down from the roof of his palace and saw her washing herself and saw that she was beautiful to look upon. Now, when a person washes theirself, they have their clothes off, and in witchcraft, there is a love spell that's cast by letting a person see them naked. Bathsheba knew David was king, and while he was walking around looking down from his roof, he happened to see her naked, washing herself. She knew he was up there and planned for him to look down and see her naked. When David caught sight of her, she looked up at him and smiled, and at that moment, the spell was cast, and David had to have her. That's not in the Bible, but that's what happened," said Arthur.

"How in dha hell can you say dhat's what happened when you weren't dhere?" asked Bob.

"He's got a good point," said Ron.

Arthur spoke up and said, "The same way you can say anything happened in the Bible when you weren't there, the same way you believe the sun went ten degrees backwards when you know it's impossible, or that Moses parted the Red Sea, or Jesus walked on water. You believe it happened because it's written in the Bible. The facts are irrelevant; it happened because we believe it happened, and that's what's called faith. Having faith is when you believe in something irregardless of when science and the facts say different things."

"If that's the case, our beliefs outweigh the facts," said Grandfather. "And if the facts are irrelevant, then what we believe is what governs the way we live, not the facts that determine reality?"

"Okay," said Ron, "In that case, where did God come from?"

For a brief moment, the stillness of silence hung in the air, and no one said anything. Then Bob spoke up and said, "God is dha alpha and dha omega; he's dha beginning and dha end. God has always been. He created dha universe and everything in it. Before God created dha universe, nothing existed."

"That's bullshit," said Grandfather. "Everything that exists has a point, or rather a moment, when it came into existence, and that includes God, whether he exists as a concept or a real being. You claim nothing existed before God created the universe. Think about that. In order for God to exist before the universe was created, it would mean God had to exist when there was nothing in existence.

"If you take away the universe, you'll take away God along with it, and nothing will exist because the universe is everything. But if you take away God, the universe and everything in it will still exist."

Bob became angry at Grandfather, and everyone in the station wagon could tell Bob was upset. As the station wagon approached the corner where the prostitutes were standing, the traffic light in front of Grandfather changed from green to yellow. Grandfather did not want to stop at the light because he knew the prostitutes on the corner would wave at them and try to attract their attention.

Just seeing them reminded him that his daughter Esther was a prostitute and did the same thing they did. He was not sure if he could make the yellow light and was about to slow down and stop for the red light when Bob spoke up and said, "Ain't dat your daughter Esther out dere standing on da corner?" He quickly corrected himself and said, "No, it ain't her. For a moment, I thought it was Esther. She looked just like her."

When Bob said that, Grandfather hit the gas pedal, putting the accelerator to the floor. All he could think of was making it into the intersection before the light turned red. But the light turned red just as the front wheels of the vehicle were about to enter the intersection. When Grandfather entered the intersection, he knew the light was red, but the station wagon was going too fast to stop. As soon as the station wagon entered the intersection, a huge big rig slammed into it, crushing the entire driver's side of the vehicle. In less than an instant, the station wagon was airborne. Brooms, mops, and mop buckets were flying about inside the station wagon, along with cleaning supplies. The vehicle completely rolled over and landed in the lane of oncoming traffic in the opposite direction of the big rig that slammed into it. As soon as the station wagon landed in the lane of oncoming traffic, it was hit by another vehicle that literally tore the station wagon wide open. It was almost cut in half. Bob was the only survivor.

****

Grandfather found himself in total darkness, trying to remember anything he could. At first, he couldn't remember anything—not even his name, who he was, or where he was. He seemed to be sitting in a huge movie theater, the largest movie theater he could imagine. Sitting next to him was Arthur on one side and Ron on the other. The theater was entirely full of people; there was not one empty seat. It was completely dark at first, but little by little, his eyes seemed to adjust to the darkness. Grandfather remembered his name. "Geary," he said to himself, "My name is Geary McAllister."

As soon as Grandfather remembered his name, the motion picture appeared on the screen. It was the story of his life. He found himself watching a movie that was about his whole life. At first, Grandfather couldn't remember a thing, but as his memory began to come back to him, he could see it projected on the screen in front of him. Whatever he remembered was shown in the movie theater. This was the case with everyone in the theater; they were all looking at what they could remember of their lives.

Grandfather sat there and watched his whole life up until the time he ran a red light, got hit by a big rig, and was killed. By now, he realized he was dead. He understood he was no longer inside a physical body. Once everyone in the theater finished watching their life stories, they were able to communicate with each other without using words. Their consciousness began to merge into one another, becoming a collective consciousness where everyone knew what one another was thinking. It was similar to watching a huge flock of small birds, numbering in the thousands, all flying across the sky in the same direction, making the same maneuvers without telling one another which way to go—just reacting to the current of wind that carried them.

Grandfather was no longer Geary McAllister because Geary McAllister was just a label. It was the name of the physical body he used to be in, not the consciousness inside that body. The name Geary McAllister would become a memory of a person made of flesh and blood, once a container, a vessel for his consciousness to dwell inside somewhere in the past. The saying, "I have consciousness; therefore, I exist," seemed more profound to him now than it ever did while he was inside the physical body of a human being.

Now, he was no longer a human being; he was no longer alive, and yet he still existed. He thought about the religious beliefs not just of the people he had known when he was alive but also the beliefs of the collective consciousness he was now a part of. As he explored his newfound consciousness, he realized that each and every person who died at the same time he did had found themselves in a place where their consciousness merged into one collective consciousness.

All had something in common: they all had a soul. Everyone is born with a soul, but not everyone has one when they die. He remembered asking what the difference was between the spirit and a soul many years ago when he used to go to church. Now, he could feel the difference. The soul and the spirit were interchangeable, but there was a huge difference. The brain and the mind are two different things that work together as one physical element, like the difference between the engine and the transmission in an automobile. The engine supplies the power, while the transmission transfers that power to turn the wheels of the automobile and make it go.

The spirit is the spark of life, the basic energy that gives life to every living thing on Earth. In contrast, the soul is the guiding force that directs that energy and determines which way to go. The spirit does not have consciousness, but the soul is aware of the consciousness inside a human being and is a part of that consciousness. He and everyone else could feel the power of their spirit, propelling them to a higher level of consciousness.

There is a story on Earth about the Buddha and how he sat under a tree to attain enlightenment. The enlightenment he achieved came from within him; it was already in him before he sat down. This was similar to what happened to a person's consciousness after they died. They received enlightenment, which raised their consciousness to a much higher level than they could ever perceive or achieve as human beings. As he became aware of this higher level of consciousness, he could feel the entire state of consciousness he was part of moving to a higher level.

As they all moved to this higher level, they could feel the space they were leaving behind becoming occupied by the consciousness of people who had just died and were no longer in their physical bodies. At the same time, their own consciousness seemed to be growing. They were becoming part of a consciousness that existed before they died or before they were born, which caused them to move into another realm on a higher level where their consciousness expanded, becoming much more prolific as entities that existed on a spiritual level.

He remembered a story about what the crucifix was supposed to represent. If the image of Jesus was on the cross, the crucifix represented the Son of God dying for our sins. If the crucifix did not have the image of Jesus on it and was just a cross with nothing on it, it symbolized the two dimensions in which we live: one is the material world, and the other is the spiritual world that coincides with the material world on a superficial level of existence. The vertical part of the cross represents the spiritual world, while the horizontal part represents the material world.

There is a place where the vertical and horizontal parts of the cross meet at an axis to form a juncture. This spot on the cross represents where the spiritual world and the material world meet and become one. It symbolizes reality at its most profound nature, indicating that one world does not exist completely by itself without the other. Together, both the material world and the spiritual world are the determining factors of the reality we live in, and the place where the two worlds meet is the highest criterion of reality.

That no longer applied. He was in a space and time that did not have mass. When he first arrived and found himself sitting in a darkened theater, he had a sense of being in a space with no time. But after he became part of the collective consciousness and began to move to a higher plane of existence, he felt as if the restrictions of space and time had slowly disappeared. Time was no longer relevant, and space seemed more like a concept than a real thing, for the world he was in did not have matter.

When he was in the darkened theater watching his life on the motion picture screen, he could feel all the emotions he experienced when he was alive. However, after moving to a higher level of consciousness, his emotions no longer seemed to exist. He no longer felt emotion; instead, logic became his primary source of motivation. He could see all of his emotions for what they were. It was as if a person wearing an overcoat on a cold or rainy day stepped inside a warm house, and the first thing they did was remove their overcoat. He could see human emotion as that overcoat he had just taken off and hung in the closet.

He could see fear, hatred, envy, jealousy, joy, pride, sadness, embarrassment, shame, guilt, and many other emotions that once seemed essential to life, yet now appeared useless. The most profound and seemingly useless emotion, however, was love. Love can never be truly understood while one walks the earth as a human being. All human beings have spiritual needs as well as material needs: food, water, and shelter are material needs; success, pride, and achievements are spiritual needs. And love is the greatest spiritual need of all. Love acts as a conduit to the spiritual world. There is a connection that love somehow creates between the spiritual and material worlds. Yet, when a person dies and no longer exists as a human being, love is no longer needed.

For a while, he felt as if his state of existence depended on either reaching the next level of consciousness or being drawn back down to a lower level in the spiritual world—a level where every soul is eventually reborn as a human being. He and everyone else in the collective consciousness still had their souls, but now came a time when either he would return to a lower level and be reborn as a human being or rise to a higher level, where at some point, his soul would merge into what some call God, or the highest level of consciousness that exists.

At this juncture, a distinct difference became evident among the souls. The souls of people who had been vegans and vegetarians seemed to excel to the next higher level of consciousness effortlessly, while the souls of those who ate meat struggled, unable to escape an earth-like gravity that kept them from rising to a higher level of existence without profound effort.

For him, it wasn't about free will, though he knew he had a choice. It felt more like the universe had a designated place for him to be. He could feel his soul being pulled in a certain direction. In that direction, there were more souls than he could imagine. Three worlds seemed to exist simultaneously, each made up of different kinds of souls.

The first world was composed of the souls of those who had faith in God. The second world contained the souls of people who believed in something but did not believe in God as the church or any religion proclaimed. They often referred to a "higher power" when speaking of a supreme being, but most importantly, they believed in a spiritual existence and life after death. The third world was made up of the souls of people who did not believe in God and believed that death marked the end of existence.

He found himself in the second world, where, far off in the distance, he could hear the faint sound of a heartbeat. The heartbeat grew louder and louder, and as it did, the consciousness of his soul began to dissipate. He was on his way to being reborn as another human being.

THE END